Merlyn Hated Him Immediately.

Of course, he couldn't have known that she'd be standing in the middle of the hall at twelve o'clock at night. On the other hand, she hadn't expected him to blow in from a horrible thunderstorm and knock her down on the carpet.

"Why don't you watch where you're going?" she shot at him. "You were moving like a freight train!"

The eyes she couldn't quite see under his heavy eyebrows seemed to throw off sparks. "Who the hell are you?" he demanded, moving toward her.

"Now, now," she cautioned, stumbling backward. "Temper, temper. You'll hurt yourself."

"Not damned likely," he said darkly, and kept coming.

DIANA PALMER

is a native Georgian and a newspaper reporter. She married her husband, James, after a five-day courtship and they now have a son. They are still newly-weds, having been married only eleven years. They live with two arrogan_____ th east Georgia town, w_____ time planting flowers chasing unicorns.

Dear Reader:

SILHOUETTE DESIRE is an exciting new line of contemporary romances from Silhouette Books. During the past year, many Silhouette readers have written in telling us what other types of stories they'd like to read from Silhouette, and we've kept these comments and suggestions in mind in developing SILHOUETTE DESIRE.

DESIREs feature all of the elements you like to see in a romance, plus a more sensual, provocative story. So if you want to experience all the excitement, passion and joy of falling in love, then SILHOUETTE DESIRE is for you.

Meredith Morgan,
Silhouette Books,
320 Steelcase Rd., East,
Markham, Ontario
L3R 2M1

DIANA PALMER
Lady Love

 Silhouette Desire

Published by Silhouette Books New York

Distributed in Canada by PaperJacks Ltd., a Licensee
of the trademarks of Simon & Schuster, Inc.

For Shirley and Cordia

SILHOUETTE BOOKS, a Division of Simon & Schuster, Inc.
1230 Avenue of the Americas, New York, N.Y. 10020
In Canada distributed by PaperJacks Ltd.,
330 Steelcase Road, Markham, Ontario

Distributed by Pocket Books

ISBN: 0-671-49600-X

First Silhouette Books printing December, 1984

10 9 8 7 6 5 4 3 2 1

Printed in Canada

Books by Diana Palmer

Silhouette Romance

Darling Enemy #254
Roomful of Roses #301
Heart of Ice #314
Passion Flower #328

Silhouette Special Edition

Heather's Song #33

Silhouette Desire

The Cowboy and the Lady #12
September Morning #26
Friends and Lovers #50
Fire and Ice #80
Snow Kisses #102
Diamond Girl #110
The Rawhide Man #157
Lady Love #175

Lady Love

1

Merlyn Forrest Steele's eyes were the same shade of green as her father's, but Jared Steele's had a twinkle that, at the moment, she was too angry to match. She glared at him from the plush white depths of the horseshoe-shaped sofa, its covering emphasizing the jet blackness of her long hair.

"It's all your fault," she told him shortly.

His eyebrows arched. "What is?"

"Adam."

He gave a world-weary sigh and stuck his hands deep in the pockets of his charcoal gray suit pants. His silver mustache twitched as he frowned. "I see what you mean," he confessed. "I meant well."

"I didn't mean your matchmaking attempts," she explained. Her hand smoothed a wrinkle in her green silk slacks. "I meant the fact that you're so rich."

"I often think of donating my fortune to charity and throwing myself on the mercy of strangers," he murmured, tongue-in-cheek.

She glared at him again. "I never know if it's me or your money that men want," she said. "Adam seemed to be head over heels in love with me, and I was . . . warming to him. Then I found out that he only got engaged to me because he had dreams of becoming your business partner! Now where in the world did he get an idea like that? Especially since he works for a rival computer company!"

Her father turned away and looked out the window. "Look at that sun," he said with enthusiasm. "Imagine, it's spring already!"

"Evading the issue, huh?" she challenged.

He hunched his shoulders and glanced at her. "Well, darling, you aren't ugly," he reminded her.

"I'm not poor, either—that's the trouble."

"He seemed like a good prospect," her father murmured defensively.

So he had, Merlyn thought. Her father had introduced her to Adam James at a party. Jared Steele felt that, at twenty-six, his only child was ripe for the joys of wedded bliss. So for the past year he'd been flinging unsuspecting males at Merlyn's feet in what she considered a pathetically obvious way. If her mother had still been alive, perhaps her father would have been too occupied to bother Merlyn. But, as it was, he was determined to marry her off, and no eligible bachelor of reasonable means escaped his eagle eye.

Adam James had seemed to be a prize catch. A minor executive in a rival computer company, he had come to Jared's attention at a computer conference.

Her father had dragged him home to Merlyn as proudly as a hunting dog carrying a duck in its mouth.

Adam, for his part, had seemed immediately smitten and had pursued Merlyn with considerable enthusiasm. Right up until the very end, she'd been fooled by his persuasive charm, despite the fact that only her mind agreed to the liaison. Her body had been ice-cold in his arms; somehow, he'd never managed to stir her. No man had managed that in her virginal life, although she was certain she had passion in her. She loved fast cars and excitement and all sorts of hobbies that her father had predicted would be the death of her.

She hadn't gotten over Adam in the month since their engagement had been broken. She'd gone off to France for two weeks and come back with a suntan, a sour disposition, and a grudge against her disappointed parent. Now she was bored again, and nagging him had become a rather satisfying diversion for her.

"I want to be loved for myself," she muttered.

His eyebrows arched again. "I love you."

"Prove it," she challenged. "Stop throwing men at me!"

He threw up his hands. "My God, all I want is a few grandchildren!"

"Adopt!"

He glowered at her. "Shame on you, moaning over being rich. Plenty of women would love to walk in your shoes."

"Maybe I'd like to be poor for a change!" she shot back, rising from the sofa. "And have a chance to be liked for myself alone."

"So, do it," he dared her, with narrowed eyes. "I dare you. If you think it's so wonderful being poor, you go try it. I grew up with nothing, but you've always had the advantages. Let's see you get along without them. For, say, a month." His eyes twinkled mischievously and he wiggled his mustache, which had more hair in it than he had on his head. "Live without money. Work for your keep. And if you can manage that for a month, without telling anyone who you are or what you're worth, I'll swear off matchmaking for life. Cross my heart."

She pursed her lips, and her own green eyes began to twinkle. "A month, huh?"

"A month."

"What kind of work could I do?"

"You've got a degree in history," he reminded her.

"Lots of people have."

He looked thoughtful. "Yes, but I think I know a way you could use it."

She cocked her head warily. "Oh, no, you don't."

"No men," he said, holding up his hands defensively. "Just a lovely lady who writes torrid historical romances. She lives on Lake Lanier, north of here."

"In Gainesville?" she asked, and he nodded. She studied him. "What would I do?"

"Help her with some research on her next book. Jack Thomas was talking about it yesterday. We were at the board meeting of that college—you know, we're both trustees. He knows Cameron Thorpe, the Charleston banker, well. The writer is Thorpe's mother. She lives alone, except for a housekeeper."

It was sounding better and better to Merlyn. She knew Lake Lanier. It was a man-made lake, Georgia's biggest, and one of her good friends raced at Road Atlanta near there. Dick Langley had an enormous home on the lake, which she'd visited occasionally.

"She's a writer?" She frowned. "Does she write under her own name?"

"No. Her given name is Lila Thorpe," he said, "but she writes as Copper O'Mara."

She gasped. "But I read her!" she burst out. "She's one of my favorites!"

"All the more reason to apply for the job," he chuckled. "Want me to call Jack Thomas and ask if he knows her phone number? And don't worry, I won't blow your cover. I'll say I have an acquaintance who might qualify for the job."

"Fair enough," she said. "I'll show you I'm no society darling."

He studied her slenderness and smiled with pure pride. "You've got class, though. Just like your mother."

"But she was beautiful," Merlyn argued.

He nodded. "The most beautiful creature on earth. I still miss her, you know." He turned away. "Well, let's get this show on the road, daughter." He picked up the phone.

Three days later, on a rainy Friday, Merlyn drove up to the large two-story lake house where Lila Thorpe lived. It was a fieldstone and wood building as beautiful as its natural surroundings. Beyond it was the lake, with a boathouse and a private cove and pier. Around it was open land, with hills and pine trees and none of the cluttered construction one found closer in to Gainesville.

Merlyn imagined that the estate would be beautiful in the sun, and she could hardly wait for the weather to break and the warm breezes to herald blossoming things. There were dogwood trees all around the house, along with small shrubs; the dogwoods were in bud already.

She carried her suitcase up to the front porch and rang the doorbell. A small, thin woman in a cotton dress let her in.

"I'm Tilly," she introduced herself. "Mrs. Thorpe is in the living room. If you'll follow me?"

There was a quick scurrying sound on the staircase in the long hall. Merlyn got a glimpse of a dark-haired, dark-eyed girl of about twelve who hesitated a few steps up.

"Hello." Merlyn grinned, tossing back her long black hair. "I'm Merlyn Forrest," she said, deliberately leaving off the "Steele."

The child, obviously shy, stared at her, unsmiling. "Hello," she said after a minute.

"This is a lovely house," Merlyn said. "Do you live here with Mrs. Thorpe?"

"She's my grandmother."

How formal the child sounded, how repressed. Why did she live with her grandmother? Where were her parents? Was Cameron Thorpe, the man her father had mentioned, this little girl's father?

"This way, Miss," Tilly called when she realized that Merlyn was lagging behind.

"Yes, excuse me," Merlyn said. She winked at the girl and walked on.

Lila Thorpe was tall, thin and graying and had twinkling eyes. She held out a slender hand to shake

Merlyn's extended one. "You must be Merlyn," she said, smiling. "I'm so glad you're here! I simply can't research and write at the same time, and I have this incredible pull toward English royalty at the moment. What do you know about the Plantagenets and the Tudors?"

Merlyn caught her breath with a little laugh. "In fact, just a smattering, though the English kings have always fascinated me. But I brought my history books along, and I can find anything you need. How about that?"

"Perfect!" Lila sighed.

"Is she going to live here?" the little girl asked from the doorway.

Merlyn turned and found the child hesitating at the door. She was wearing a white and brown cotton frock, knee-high socks, and patent leather shoes. She had a manner that was much older than her years, and eyes that didn't smile.

"Yes," Lila said warmly. "Come in, Amanda, and meet Merlyn Forrest. She's going to help me research my new book."

"She told me her name in the hall," Amanda murmured.

"Yes, I did, but you didn't tell me yours," Merlyn said warmly. "Did you know that Amanda means 'worthy of love'? It was my mother's middle name."

The child's huge eyes widened. "Really?" Her shoulders hunched. "My mother is dead."

"So is mine," Merlyn said with quiet sympathy. "It's rather lonely, isn't it? At least you have your grandmother."

Amanda tilted her head, studying the newcomer.

15

Merlyn was wearing jeans and a velour pullover. She had purposely avoided designer pieces, choosing instead clothes in some medium price range that wouldn't arouse suspicion. But with her usual flair, she was wearing a vibrant Mexican poncho over the outfit. She looked colorful and bright and a little nonconformist.

"That's so pretty," Amanda remarked of the poncho. "It's like a rainbow."

"I got it . . . I mean, a friend brought it to me from Mexico," Merlyn said. In fact, it had been purchased by Merlyn herself in Mexico City, but it wouldn't do to let them know how well traveled she was. She grinned. "I'll let you wear it sometime, if you like."

Amanda brightened, and then her face fell and she shrugged. "Daddy wouldn't let me," she muttered. "He won't even let me wear jeans. He's afraid I'll grow up to be a tomboy."

Daddy sure must be weird, Merlyn thought, but she didn't say anything.

"My son is a banker," Lila confided. "My only living child. There was another boy, but he was stillborn. Cam is all I have now. His wife died some years ago."

Odd wording, Merlyn thought as Tilly brought coffee and cake on a tray and interrupted the conversation. It was strange that Lila hadn't called her late daughter-in-law by name. But that was none of her business, and she wasn't the interfering sort. The son sounded awful. She was glad he didn't live at the lake house. For an instant she had feared that her father might be matchmaking again, but she quickly dismissed the idea. Cameron Thorpe probably looked like Dracula. Certainly he sounded like him.

Merlyn and Lila spent a pleasant afternoon getting to know each other. Surprisingly, Amanda stayed with them; she seemed drawn to Merlyn. Merlyn felt a tug of affection herself, because she'd been lonely like that after her mother's death, when her father had buried himself in his work and had no time for her. Perhaps that was Amanda's problem, too.

By bedtime Merlyn had some idea of Lila's working schedule and the scope of the project. She pored over her texts before she went to bed, seeking out bits and pieces of information to give Lila the next morning.

She liked her room. It overlooked the lake and featured French Provincial furniture, right down to the canopied bed and a blue and white color scheme. Already she felt at home. She was going to prove to her father once and for all that she could make it without his fortune. After Adam, she wanted no more attempts at matchmaking.

Adam. Funny, when he'd let it slip that he expected to become her father's business partner at the same time that he became her husband, she hadn't really been heartbroken. She didn't even cry when he made it clear that the marriage wouldn't take place without the partnership. Her pride was hurt much more than her heart.

She sighed and put Adam out of her mind. She couldn't seem to settle down that night. Perhaps it was the new environment, the unfamiliar surroundings. Or maybe it was the thunderstorm raging outside. She got up to make herself a cup of hot chocolate. Maybe a warm drink would help her to sleep.

Out in the hallway, it was pitch black. It must be

close to midnight, Merlyn thought. The rest of the household was asleep. The darkness was sporadically lit by flashes of lightning from the storm. Getting her bearings during one of the lightning bursts, she hurried down the hall, turned the corner and ran headlong into a formidable barrier.

2

Merlyn hated him immediately. Of course, he couldn't have known that she'd be standing in the middle of the hall in the dark at twelve o'clock at night. On the other hand, she hadn't expected him to blow in out of a horrible thunderstorm and knock her down onto the thick pile carpet.

"Of all the . . ." came a voice as black and deep as thunder rumbling. "Who the hell are you?"

She threw back her long black hair. The next lightning flash caught her glaring into a face that would have gone well with a copy of *Jane Eyre* and antique furniture.

He was big. Bigger than any man she'd ever met face to face. Tall, built like a wrestler. Hands like hams, holding a black attaché case and an umbrella. He wasn't wearing a hat, and his hair was thick and black and bushy and needed trimming. He was wearing a blue pin-striped suit, and the eyes she couldn't quite see under his heavy eyebrows seemed to throw off sparks.

"Why don't you watch where you're going?" she shot back, too shaken to get up. "You were moving like a freight train! Come to think of it," she added darkly, "you look a little like one."

"Get up from there."

"Yes, sir!" she said smartly, glaring at him as she pulled herself to her feet. She didn't like the way he was looking at her, so she pulled the thin blue robe closer around her slender, half-clad body. Her feet were bare; she hadn't thought about slippers. She hadn't even brought any, come to think of it.

"Well?" he growled.

"That," she said with a sweet smile, "is a deep subject. And you look like a man with a shallow mind. Were you invited, or are you a cat burglar?" She looked him up and down. He was doing a great impression of a man about to explode. "Make that an elephant burglar. Boy, I'd love to see you try to sneak up on somebody."

Her grin didn't seem to impress him much. He slammed the attaché case to the floor. "Who the hell are you?"

"Miss Jane Eyre, sir," she said, making him a sweeping curtsy. "I've come to tutor the youngster and provide romantic interest for you."

"Oh, my God, I don't believe this," he muttered, running a hand over his unshaven face. "Six hours on airplanes, two waiting in baggage claim . . . Lady, unless you want to spend what's left of the night in the nearest police station, you'd damned well better come up with some quick answers."

"There's a phone in the living room," she suggested. "I'll look up the number for you."

He moved forward, and she moved backward. "Now, now," she cautioned, stumbling. "Temper, temper. You'll hurt yourself."

"Not damned likely," he said darkly, and kept coming.

"Mrs. Thorpe!" Merlyn screamed, and went tearing off down the hall toward that lady's room.

"What?" Lila appeared in her doorway, looking disheveled and drowsy. She gaped at Merlyn cowering against the wall, and then at the big, angry man almost on her.

"Cameron!" she exclaimed, a smile appearing on her lined face. "Well, what an unexpected delight on a horrible evening like this. Come here and let me look at you, dear!

"I see you've already met Merlyn Forrest," she continued, smiling at the younger woman pressed against the wall. "Merlyn, this is my son, Cameron."

"Your son?" Merlyn blinked. "This is your son?" She stared at the man, who was easily twice his mother's weight and the exact opposite of her fair coloring.

"Who is she?" Cameron Thorpe asked coldly.

"Now, dear . . ." his mother began.

"Who?"

"Merlyn Forrest," Lila said, exasperated. "Don't you remember that I was looking for someone to help me do some research on my new book?"

He stared at Merlyn as if he couldn't imagine that she had enough brains to be able to read.

"How did you find her?" he asked curtly.

"In the Yellow Pages," Merlyn murmured, "under 'brilliant research associates.'"

He gave her a hard look. "Mother?" he persisted.

Lila sighed. "A friend of yours, in fact, that Jack Thomas. He knew someone who knew someone . . ."

"Does she have credentials?" he asked with a suspicious glance at Merlyn.

"I have a B.A. in history," Merlyn said sweetly. "And pretending hostility toward me will not work, sir. You and I were obviously meant for each other—you just won't admit it." She batted her long eyelashes demurely. "It was like lightning striking, when our eyes met. . . ."

He muttered something she was glad she didn't really hear, and went back to pick up his umbrella and attaché case.

Lila was trying not to smile. "Cameron, don't you dare try to scare off my new assistant," she said after a minute. "I can't do this book alone, and I have to have Merlyn for the next month at least."

"A month?" He looked hunted.

"She'll be company for Amanda and me," Lila said shortly. "Amanda likes her."

So this was the little girl's father, Merlyn thought. Cameron the Cold Heart. He did fit the image of a businessman who was all business all the time. No wonder the little girl looked so repressed. She didn't have a chance with a father like that. She studied

Cameron Thorpe quietly and wondered how he'd look in red polka-dotted boxer shorts. She had to bite her lip hard to keep from bursting out laughing.

"I thought children were supposed to be perceptive," he muttered.

Merlyn gave him the once-over and tugged her blue robe closer. "I'm so glad you like me, Mr. Thorpe," she sighed theatrically. She grinned. "I like you, too. Dark, somber men really turn me on."

Once again, he looked as though he might explode. His mother, kind soul, moved quickly in front of Merlyn.

"Now, dear," she told Cameron gently, "it's late and you must be tired. Why don't you get some rest? Can you stay the entire weekend?"

"Yes," he said. "And if you could keep Jane Eyre here out of sight while my guests are in residence . . . ?"

"Guests?" Lila asked.

"Charlotte and Delle Radner," he said. "They're coming up from Atlanta tomorrow."

Lila sighed. "Oh." She didn't look enthusiastic. "Of course, your friends are welcome."

"You'll get used to them," he promised her with a slight softening.

"I suppose I'll have to," came the resigned reply.

"I suppose one of them is your girlfriend," Merlyn said, letting her full lips pout at him. "Well, I want you to know that my heart is broken, just broken. And I did love you at first sight . . . uh, what was your name again?"

He started to speak, then sliced the air with that big

hand, turned on his heel and stomped off down the hall with steps heavy enough to rattle the glass in the windows.

Lila collapsed in muffled laughter. Tears welled in her eyes. "Oh, Merlyn, you're so good for me. I've never seen him like that before."

"I don't imagine many people have," Merlyn mused, glancing down the deserted hall. "My goodness, he frightened me to death when he came storming in. I remembered that you had a son, but you hadn't mentioned that he'd be coming tonight."

"I'd forgotten, in the excitement of your arrival," Lila replied with a smile. "He did drop a hint that he might invite Delle and her mother up for the weekend while they were visiting relatives in Atlanta. It's not far, you know." She looked momentarily worried. "Charlotte Radner—here." She sighed heavily. "I can hardly believe she'd actually brave the great outdoors long enough to blemish her white skin."

"Which one is the girlfriend?" Merlyn asked hesitantly.

"Delle," came the hard reply. "She's mama's little girl. Oh, my, the Radners—here. And I did so want to start work tomorrow. . . . No matter. We'd better get some sleep, dear. Maybe we can work around them."

"I've been doing some preliminary research tonight," Merlyn said as they walked down the hall together. "I think I've found you a feisty period in the founding of the Tudor line. Would that suit?"

Lila's eyes brightened. "Perfect! I can save the Plantagenets for another book. By all means, let's start there. In the morning we can start laying out the plot. This is going to be great fun," she said with a smile.

"I hope so," Merlyn said dryly, glancing down the hall where Cameron Thorpe had disappeared.

"Don't worry, you and I will be a match for him," Lila promised. "I just wish that once or twice he'd come alone and spend some time with Amanda. He's only here on the weekends, and she's been with me most of her life. Cameron divorced her mother years ago, and he got custody, but he lives in Charleston and he really doesn't have anyone else to leave her with. . . . Her mother's dead now, as you know."

"Why can't Delle keep her?" Merlyn asked matter-of-factly.

Lila looked horrified. "Delle? Look after a child?"

"Sorry," Merlyn murmured. She was beginning to get an interesting picture of Cameron's so-called friends.

"I'm sorry that Cameron upset you," Lila said, letting the subject of Delle drop, as though it bothered her.

"In all fairness to him," Merlyn replied, "he couldn't have expected to find me wandering the halls. I was going to make myself a cup of hot chocolate, but after all this excitement, I'm so exhausted I think I'll be able to sleep without it."

"You'll love it here when the rains stop," Lila promised. "I've lived on the lake for four years now, and I can't imagine living anywhere else. It's so peaceful. And when the weather begins to get warm, as it will be soon, there will be sailboats dotting the lake."

"I've seen the lake from the road many times," Merlyn murmured, not wanting to mention her friend Dick's enormous house, which was right on the lake.

"It provides drinking water for Atlanta and the metro area, as well as being a marvelous recreational facility. Isn't that right?"

Lila smiled. "My, you seem quite familiar with the area already. Sleep well, my dear."

"You, too."

Merlyn shot one last glance down the hall before she went into her room and quickly closed the door. Talk about flies in the ointment! Cameron Thorpe was going to be trouble, and she had a feeling that his lady friends were going to foul things up, too. All her confidence in being able to maintain her new identity was draining away. She'd have to be on her guard every minute, or she'd blow her cover. It looked as if this job wasn't going to be the plum she'd first expected it to be.

Well, she thought with a sigh, as she climbed into bed and pulled up the covers, perhaps things will improve tomorrow.

They didn't. The next morning, which dawned clear and warm, Cameron Thorpe was sitting at the breakfast table on the patio with his mother when Merlyn walked in. The look he gave her would have stopped traffic.

His dark eyes—they were almost black at close range, deep-set under a jutting brow—ran up and down Merlyn's slender figure. She was dressed in faded blue jeans and a flaming orange pullover T-shirt that read "Kiss me, I'm a frog!" Her long black hair fell over her shoulders, and her eyes were a pale, sparkling green. She wasn't beautiful like her late mother, but she had delicate features and a perfect figure, and normally she dressed with a flair that set her apart. Today, however, she'd deliberately worn her most outlandish T-shirt, hoping to get a rise out of Mr. Conservative. And she did. Immediately.

"Do you normally dress like that?" Cameron asked.

"Why, yes, when I'm not going naked," she replied with a careless smile. She stared at him. He was wearing a dark business suit with a dark tie and a white shirt. She'd have bet that he had a closet full of them, all alike.

"More eggs, Cameron?" Lila asked quickly as Merlyn sat down and helped herself to toast and coffee.

"No, thanks," he said, and his eyes never left Merlyn. His face was broad and hard, his no was formidable, and he had a jaw as square as the   ay he dressed.

"Sizing me up?" Merlyn asked. "I wea size ten slacks and a medium T-shirt. And there nothing underneath," she whispered, leaning forward.

He came as close to a flush as she'd ever seen a man come, and his black eyes glittered at her. "I don't find your attitude amusing," he said curtly. "And I won't have my daughter subjected to remarks like that."

"Amanda isn't downstairs yet," Merlyn told him, "and you're hardly a child." She studied him. "Mrs. Thorpe said you were a banker."

"Yes," he said, sounding as if he found speaking to her distasteful.

"How exciting," she murmured, stifling a yawn.

"Where did you take your degree?" he asked out of the blue.

"The University of Georgia."

"Did you specialize?" he persisted, as he sipped his coffee.

"Not really," she returned. "I enjoy ancient history as well as other periods."

"What qualifies you to be a research assistant?" he chided. "Do you have references?"

"Are you the reincarnation of the Spanish Inquisition?" she shot back. "Really, Mr. Thorpe, my qualifications satisfied your mother."

"They certainly did," Lila seconded. She frowned. "Cameron, I've never known you to be so rude to a guest!"

"We've never had a guest like this," he said, glancing up and down Merlyn's figure.

"How sad for you." Merlyn smiled. "But, at long last, here I am!"

"I've got to make a phone call," he muttered, glaring at Merlyn as he got to his feet. "Five more minutes of Jane Eyre there, and I'll be searching for a blunt instrument."

"How kinky," Merlyn said, grinning. "Usually men are wildly excited when they get to that point. Are you by any chance trying to seduce me over the scrambled eggs?"

His mother had already turned away with a napkin over her mouth.

"If I were eighty with terminal acne, I wouldn't be so desperate," he replied.

"You'll be heartbroken when you realize what you're passing up," Merlyn called after him.

The hall door slammed behind him, and Lila made strangled sounds in her napkin.

"Poor Cameron," Lila said finally. "He's so domineering with women."

"Not this one," Merlyn informed her smugly. "I'm a free spirit. Basically, I hate men."

"Is there a reason?"

Merlyn smiled. "Yes. A fiancé who turned out to be Dracula. I broke the engagement, and now I'm trying to get myself back together."

"I'm sorry."

"So am I," Merlyn said. "I was ready to settle down. I'm twenty-six, after all. I wouldn't mind a husband and children. But it's going to take some time to forget what happened."

"You're still young, my dear," Lila said with a smile.

"So I am," Merlyn agreed. Then she changed the subject. "Where are we going to work? Inside?" she asked, casting a wary eye toward the house.

"That wouldn't be intelligent, would it?" Lila laughed. "I can see you now, hurling things at Cameron!"

"Only a few sticks of furniture," Merlyn protested. She sighed. "Don't worry, Mrs. Thorpe, I'll get used to him. After all, I got used to asparagus and squash casserole."

Lila laughed merrily. "Call me Lila, not Mrs. Thorpe. And, yes, I think you'll get used to my son, and he to you, in time. It will do him good to learn that not every woman thinks he's the final authority." She got to her feet. "Since it's so warm, we'll hash out some preliminaries here on the patio," she added. "I'll get my legal pad, and you can fetch those history books I watched you lug up the staircase yesterday."

"I'll get them right now," Merlyn said.

Minutes later she came back downstairs with an armload of books, fortunately without running into the lord of the manor.

"Amanda's late this morning," Merlyn remarked as she seated herself at the little white table.

"Yes, but not unusually so," Lila said with a smile. She sat down across from Merlyn. "With school out for spring holidays, she doesn't get up until eleven." She sighed, and the smile faded. "Poor child, she's so lonely. Cameron has very little time . . ."

"He could make time, if he wanted to," Merlyn said quietly. "My own childhood was lonely. My mother died when I was about Amanda's age, and my father missed her terribly. Instead of turning to me, he turned to his work. It wasn't until I was well into my teens that he suddenly discovered he was a parent. We've grown closer, but there was quite a gulf between us during those first few years without Mama."

"I'm afraid that Cameron's work is his whole life," Lila said. She stared at her slender, elegant hand on the table. "His late wife was not the kind of person he needed. Marcia was wildly exciting, I suppose, but not at all domestic. She hated children. If Cameron hadn't threatened to toss her to the press, she'd have had an abortion. She left him just after Amanda was born. She was killed several years later in an automobile accident. A tragic affair, all around."

"Did Amanda know her at all?" Merlyn asked.

"No. Marcia considered Amanda a liability, not an asset. She's not the most beautiful child in the world, despite her sweet nature and kind heart. Although I doubt Marcia would have wanted her anyway. She just didn't have any maternal instinct at all."

"How sad," Merlyn said quietly. "And it's even sadder that her father gives her so little of himself. He'll regret that one day."

"He probably will. But he doesn't listen to advice, my dear."

"I noticed," Merlyn replied dryly.

"Keep right on ruffling him, Merlyn," the older woman said. "Maybe it will help."

"Oh, that doesn't take much effort—ruffling him," she assured her colleague. "I have a feeling my very existence is enough to do the trick."

They were hard at work, discussing possibilities for fictional characters during the reign of Henry VII, the founder of the Tudor line, when Amanda came downstairs. Lila was right, Merlyn thought. The little girl favored her father, and she was nobody's idea of beautiful. God bless her, she was gangly and thin and nervous, and those huge eyes swallowed her face. Probably when she grew up, she'd surprised everybody by being a beauty, though. Often it was the ugly ducklings who made the most beautiful swans— simply by taking advantage of what they had and making the most of it.

"Good morning," Merlyn said brightly, and smiled.

Amanda smiled, too. It was hard not to, when their visitor had such a contagiously sunny disposition.

"Good morning, Miss Merlyn," she said. "Good morning, Grandmama."

"Have you had breakfast?" Lila asked the child.

"No, ma'am," Amanda murmured. She sat down on the glider, her hands folded on her skirt, her long hair in neat pigtails, her blouse spotless.

"Why not?" Lila prodded.

"I didn't like to ask Mrs. Simms to fix it just for me," Amanda said shyly.

"Nonsense," Lila said. "Tilly doesn't mind. And, Amanda, it isn't as if we don't pay her. Now go and ask for what you want."

"But I'm not hungry," the child insisted.

Lila sighed heavily. "Oh, Amanda, you're just skin and bones."

"She certainly is," Cameron boomed, joining them. His dark, unsmiling eyes studied his daughter's thinness. "Get in the house and eat," he said curtly.

"Yes, Father," Amanda said in a subdued tone. She got up without raising her eyes and went back into the house.

"My, what a way you have with children, Mr. Thorpe," Merlyn said sweetly. "All the diplomacy of a rocket launcher, in fact!"

"Shut up," he told her coldly, his dark eyes daring her to make another statement.

She got to her feet. "Look here," she said, "you may order Amanda around, but I'm a big girl. I'm here to work, not to . . ."

"Then why don't you work, Miss Forrest, and leave my daughter's upbringing to me?" he asked coolly.

"Mr. Thorpe . . . !" she persisted.

"Your duties include research, I believe, Miss Forrest, not child psychology?" Cameron went on, not giving his mother a chance to interfere.

Merlyn's green eyes glittered at him. "My father used to be just like you," she said angrily. "All work, all ice. I grew up on the mercy of neighbors. I wonder how you're going to feel when Amanda is old enough to leave home, and if she'll say the same things to you that I said to my father?"

He gave her one last glare before he turned and went back into the house, slamming the door behind him.

"Oh, my," Lila murmured.

"Sorry," Merlyn grumbled as she sat back down. "He makes me so mad! I did have a lot of terrible things to say to my father at one time. We're good friends now, but we weren't always. He and your son would get along just fine."

"Yes, well, I'm sorry about all this," Lila said. "He isn't the most relaxing person to work around, even if he is my son."

"I had no right to say those things to him," Merlyn said after a minute, cooler now. "I'll apologize, if you like."

"And make him even more smug than he already is?" Lila exclaimed. "You will not!"

Merlyn laughed. "All right, then."

Amanda came back minutes later, looking puzzled yet happy. "Daddy sat with me while I had breakfast," she said. "He hasn't done that in a long time. He even talked to me."

Merlyn and Lila exchanged shocked, faintly amused glances before they got back to work.

3

Lila scribbled on a yellow legal pad and Amanda played quietly with a doll, while Merlyn dug into several volumes of information on the Tudors. But her mind was wandering, tugged away unwillingly by the conversation she'd had with Cameron earlier.

My, my, wouldn't Cameron Thorpe's eyes bulge if he could see her as she really was? She pursed her lips and fantasized about coming down the staircase of her father's town house in her white Bill Blass original with her blue fox boa draped lovingly over her bare shoulders, her hair in a high coiffure with a diamond tiara, and her mother's diamond necklace and earrings gracing her milky complexion. . . .

She shook herself. Why destroy his illusions? Let him think what he liked.

"You said the history of the English Kings had

always fascinated you. Why?" Lila asked, interrupting Merlyn's mental wanderings.

She almost told the older woman the truth—that her own family history could be traced back to the time of the Plantagenets and Tudors. But that would be giving away far too much.

"Actually, I had a cousin who was British," she said. Well, it was the truth.

"One you had a crush on?" Lila pursued.

Merlyn pursed her lips and smiled, thinking about that cousin—Richard the Lion-Hearted—and the dashing picture he made in fact and fiction. "You might say that," she agreed.

"You must tell me all about him one day." Lila sighed as she studied her notes. "This is going to be quite a feat when I really get started. I've only just roughed out the main characters. Merlyn, I'm fascinated by Uncle Jasper."

"The one who was responsible for Henry VII's accession to the throne?" Merlyn laughed delightedly. "I'm finding great material on him. During the War of the Roses, he took his brother's widow, Margaret Beaumont, to his own castle at Pembroke and provided for her while she gave birth to his nephew Henry, who was to become Henry VII—father of Henry VIII. Jasper lost his fortune in the War of the Roses, conducted something of a commando campaign against the Yorks and eventually rescued Henry Tudor from them. Henry, you see, was the last surviving male of the Lancastrian line. Their great enemies were the Yorks. Those were the two factions that fought the War of the Roses.

"But to get back to Jasper, he and Henry spent quite a while imprisoned in Brittany until the death of Edward IV, whose sons were captured by Richard III—remember him? Anyway, a faction arose to support Henry's bid for the throne, with the help of some political maneuvering by his mother, Margaret Beaumont. Uncle Jasper helped to raise an army, which marched finally into battle against Richard III. Richard was killed after a valiant defense, and Henry married Edward IV's eldest daughter, Elizabeth of York, uniting the Lancasters and Yorks and ending the War of the Roses."

Lila caught her breath. "You do have it down pat, don't you?"

"Not nearly as well as I'd like to," Merlyn confessed. "There are a lot of questions about Jasper that I haven't found answers to yet. But he seems to have lived to a ripe old age and regained his fortunes."

Lila pursed her lips and frowned. She tapped her pencil on the legal pad. "What a fascinating man. Do you suppose . . ." Her eyes cut sideways.

"Why not?" Merlyn grinned. "A fictional character patterned after him would be a natural. And the period is fascinating, as you'll see when we get further into it. I'm getting so caught up in it that I actually feel as if I can experience it in my mind."

"You should try writing," Lila told her. "I feel the same way about my fictional people and the periods they inhabit. This is the first time I've dabbled in this particular period of English history, but I'm delighted that we discovered each other."

"So am I," came the fervent reply. "I'm enjoying it more than I can tell you."

36

"I'm very glad."

"I've been a fan of yours for years," Merlyn told the older woman. "I do so enjoy the love scenes," she confessed sheepishly.

Lila laughed. "And I still do them blindfolded, because they embarrass me so!" she confessed.

"I'll bet they don't embarrass Miss Forrest," came a deep, unpleasant voice from the walkway between the rose garden and the patio.

Merlyn looked up with arched eyebrows. "Is that wishful thinking?" she asked conversationally, "because you'd like to do one with me? Well, Mr. Rochester, you're not bad-looking at all, but, honestly, I did come up here to work," she told him with a sly smile.

His eyes got darker. He was wearing a green pullover knit designer shirt with tan slacks, and despite his size he looked trim and elegant. "Are you ever serious?"

"When I balance my bank statement. It's enough to make me grim," she lied.

"Did you want something, dear?" Lila asked before the conversation had a chance to deteriorate even more.

Reluctantly, he shifted his gaze to his mother. "Delle and Charlotte are on their way up. I thought you'd like to know before they walked in. They can only stay overnight. Delle has to fly to France in the morning to join her brother in Nice for a few days."

"Lovely place, Nice," Merlyn sighed. "Blue skies, white beaches . . ."

"How would you know?" Cameron scoffed.

Oops, she thought, smiling to conceal her lapse.

"You don't believe that I might spend holidays there?" she asked innocently.

"I do not," he said bluntly, and his stare told her that he didn't think she could afford a bus ticket to Atlanta, much less a plane ticket to France.

She shrugged. "Well, then, I won't bore you with tales of summers in my father's villa there."

He ignored her. "I've asked Tilly to go to extra pains for dinner this evening," he continued. "And we'll dress. Charlotte and Delle are used to proper attire at dinner." He gave Merlyn a hard look. "They're from Charleston. Old money."

Merlyn let her jaw drop to show that she was suitably impressed.

"I would appreciate it, Miss Forrest," he added, "if you could manage to control your rather unusual sense of humor during the visit. The Radners are rather special to me."

"Oh, don't you worry, sir, I know my place," Merlyn assured him.

He looked as if he'd never smiled. Poor man, she thought, probably he never had. She wondered what he was like in bed. He probably was less adventurous than Merlyn, and Merlyn was a virgin. She grinned at the thought of Cameron without clothes.

"When I said dress," he added, "I meant formal dress."

"I have this neat sweat shirt with lace on it . . ." Merlyn began.

"But, Cameron," Lila was protesting, "Merlyn shouldn't be expected to . . ."

'Oh, really, I have plans for the evening," Merlyn

assured them, with a smile for her dark adversary. "In any case, since I came without my Bill Blass originals, it's probably for the best. Don't worry, I won't be around to embarrass you in front of the Radners. I like staying out late at night. Until the wee hours."

"Not here," he told her. "You'll be in by midnight, Miss Forrest. House rules. I don't intend having my routine interrupted by you."

She glared up at him hotly. "I will stay out as late as I like, Mr. Thorpe," she returned. "These are not Victorian times, and you are most certainly not my master. As for dressing up for dinner . . ."

"Merlyn, you are most welcome to sit down to my table naked, if you like," Lila interrupted.

"What a marvelous thought!" Merlyn laughed, rising to the occasion. She grinned at Cameron, who was getting madder by the minute. "You're turning purple," she added.

He drew in a slow breath, and his black eyes made threats. "Keep pushing," he said quietly, "and see what happens."

Her eyes widened. "I can hardly wait!"

With a harsh sigh, he turned on his heel and stalked off.

Lila grinned. "What a repressed boy I raised," she murmured. "I had such plans for Cam, but his father stole him away from me in his formative years. Being dragged around the world and ridiculed at every turn has left its mark on him, I'm afraid." She stared after him wistfully. "His father hurt him, belittled him. He wanted Cam to be strong and shrewd—well, he's that. But my husband managed to take almost all the tenderness out of him. And what he left behind, Marcia destroyed with her cruelty." She shook her head. "Cam's had a hard life. But if he marries Delle, it can only get worse."

"Is she that bad?" Merlyn asked, momentarily sympathetic.

"Oh, my dear," Lila sighed, shaking her head mournfully. "I had such high hopes that he'd settle down one day—he's nearing forty, you know. But I had hoped for a daughter-in-law who would be . . ." She glanced warily at Amanda, who was lost in her doll and its expensive accessories. ". . . different from Delle."

"Different, how?" Merlyn asked, fascinated.

"You'll see, I'm afraid," came the weary reply.

The remark turned out to be prophetic. Merlyn had already decided that the best thing for her to do would be to go into Gainesville for the rest of the day while the Radners were in residence. She'd had enough of Cameron Thorpe's disapproving glare for one day, and Lila had already told her it would be impossible to get any more work done with the guests around. The older woman had sighed wistfully when Merlyn made her decision known, and muttered that she'd like to go, too.

Merlyn walked out into the hall in her tasseled Mexican poncho with a green long-sleeved cotton blouse and white slacks, and stopped dead when she got her first look at Delle Radner.

Thin and dainty, with Shirley Temple blonde hair and over-mascaraed blue eyes, Cameron's girlfriend was dressed as if she'd just been to a cocktail party or was headed for one. Her dress was a black street-length silk charmeuse, obviously a designer model, with lavish floral lace inserts at the neckline and cuffs. Against her delicate fairness, it was devastating, and she had to know it. Her accessories were equally flawless, black snakeskin sling-back pumps and a matching purse. She was speaking to Cameron in low, girlish tones, and her full red lips were pouting up at him. Cameron, in a black dinner jacket, was looking irritated. And devastating. He would have graced the most chic establishment. Even Merlyn couldn't help feeling a ripple of pleasure at the picture he made.

She jerked herself back to reality. This man was trouble, and she wanted no part of him. Besides, she wasn't here to cozy up to Cameron the Cold. She was little more than an employee. The thought made her giggle, and she hid her mouth behind her elegantly kept hand.

The giggle drew unwanted attention. She felt two hostile pairs of eyes on her and made the most of her inbred composure. "Well, hi there," she said breathily, entering the living room with a toss of her long, exquisite hair. "You must be Delle," she told the blonde. "I've just heard so much about you!" She held out her hand, and Delle took it with a patronizing smile as her blue eyes assessed Merlyn's apparel.

"You are . . .?" Delle asked politely.

"Merlyn Forrest," Cameron supplied coldly. "She's helping my mother with a new book."

"Oh, are you a writer?" Delle's eyebrows went up.

"No. I have a degree in history," Merlyn replied.

Delle blinked. "I thought only men got those," she said with a tittering little laugh.

"Oddly enough, women do, too," Merlyn replied. She glanced at Cameron with a twitch of her lips. "Although some of them leave the halls of academia to work for striking, dark men. . . ."

"Were you going somewhere, Miss Forrest?" Cameron asked with venom in every word.

"Why, yes," she told him. "Into Gainesville to pick up men."

Lila walked in on that last mischievous statement and chuckled. "May I go, too?" she asked.

"Mother!" Cameron growled, scowling down at her.

"And who is this?" asked an icily polite voice from behind Lila.

"Merlyn Forrest, my research assistant," Lila obliged. "Merlyn, you've met Delle, of course, and this is Charlotte Radner, Delle's mother."

"Research assistant?" Charlotte laughed softly, but her eyes were as icy blue as a winter storm. She was dressed elegantly herself, in a floor-length blue dress that clung to her willowy figure. Her hair must once have been blonde, but now it was white with one of those blue rinses on it.

"Merlyn is helping me research the Plantagenet and Tudor periods for a book I'm working on," Lila offered. "Although we've almost definitely settled on the Tudors. The background is so interesting. . . ."

"I'm sure it is, dear," Charlotte said, sounding bored, "but a great many people have no taste for history, you know."

"It's so dull," Delle added, clinging to Cameron's

sleeve. "I'd rather talk about polo. Cam, are you coming down for the match next week?"

He shook his head. "I've got too much to do. There's a board meeting on a new budget."

"You never stop working," Delle complained. "Work, work, work. Why don't you come out from behind that desk and into the world? You used to play polo, I remember watching you."

"You'd have been in pigtails back then, I imagine?" Merlyn asked with a smile, noting with wicked pleasure the anger on Charlotte Radner's patrician features.

"Delle is quite mature for her age," Charlotte said coolly, curtly motioning her daughter to silence when she started to reply. "And has exquisite taste in clothes."

Merlyn spread her poncho. "And my lack of it shows?" she challenged.

Charlotte's manners wouldn't let her enter into an insult match. "My dear, I meant no offense," she said formally.

"Of course not. You wouldn't be so ill-mannered as to point out the obvious difference between your daughter's clothing budget and my own," Merlyn said.

Mrs. Radner gave her a hard glare, and Cameron's dark eyes began to glitter.

"Weren't you just leaving, Miss Forrest?" he asked, emphasizing every cold word.

"Why, yes, I was," Merlyn agreed with a grin. She tossed her dark hair like a young filly about to bolt, and her green eyes glanced off his flirtatiously. "See you."

He was openly glaring now, and Delle was giving

him funny looks. She moved closer, holding on to his arm as if he might be keeping the house from sinking.

"Have a good time, Merlyn," Lila called after her.

"I'll try to be in by two or three at the latest," Merlyn replied mischievously, with a glance toward Cameron, who'd already told her to be in by midnight. He started to say something, but before he could, Merlyn was out the door with a cheery, "Good night!"

It was a relief to breathe fresh air again. Delle was just a child, obviously infatuated with Cameron. But her mother was something else, and she held the reins on her daughter. It looked to Merlyn as if Cameron was slowly digging his own grave.

But she didn't feel the least bit sorry for him. He was cold and domineering and obviously deserved every damned thing he would get. She didn't like him. He was all the things she resented in a man. Just the thought of him made her bristle.

She walked around Lakeshore Mall for a couple of hours, haunted the B. Dalton store there, sighed over the latest computers at Radio Shack, and had supper in a charming little restaurant with hanging foliage and an uptown menu. Then she drove to the Holiday Inn, checked in, and spent the night watching movies on cable TV.

It was nine o'clock the next morning when she drove her little red Volkswagen into Lila's driveway and parked it beside Cameron's elegant black Lincoln. She glared at the larger vehicle. Black. It figured. He didn't have the personality for flashy red sports cars.

She dragged herself out of the car, still wearing the

clothes she'd worn the day before (she'd slept in her underwear) and went into the house.

Lila glanced up as she entered the dining room, smiling with something like relief. "Good morning, dear, have you eaten?"

"Not yet," Merlyn replied, with a general smile for the rest of the people at the table. Apparently Amanda was sleeping late again, but Cameron's guests were there, as elegant in pantsuits as they had been in dresses the night before. They looked as disapproving as Cameron did.

"What a lovely time I had," Merlyn sighed. She sat down beside Lila and smiled at Tilly, who poured her a cup of black coffee and pushed the platter with the buttered toast within her reach. "I hope you didn't worry?" she asked Lila.

"No, dear," Lila said with an amused smile—because she already knew that Merlyn didn't trust men and that she hadn't really spent the night picking them up.

"I was just having too much fun to come back," Merlyn sighed, munching on toast and washing it down with coffee.

"In my time," Mrs. Radner said coldly, "decent young women didn't carouse all night. Even at the age of twenty, Delle is not allowed to be out past midnight."

"You're only twenty?" Merlyn exclaimed, staring at Delle. "And you're . . . forty-five, isn't it?" she asked Cameron with pretended innocence.

"I'm thirty-nine," he said coldly.

"Nineteen years." Merlyn shook her head, glancing at Delle. "You poor child."

Cameron slammed down his napkin. "Miss Forrest . . . !" he began furiously.

"Do call me Jane, all my friends do," she told him and pursed her lips in a playful kiss.

His cheeks had a dull layer of red over them, and she was glad she wasn't alone with him.

"Cameron isn't old," Delle defended him, touching his hand lovingly. "He's in his prime. And so masterful!"

Merlyn sputtered into her coffee and almost choked. Cameron glared at her openly, clenching his fists on the table until the knuckles went white.

"My, you're in a good mood this morning, Merlyn," Lila said. "I must go with you on your next night out."

"Lila!" Mrs. Radner said curtly. "You shouldn't encourage this kind of thing. God knows, there's enough immorality in the world."

"Spending the night alone in a Holiday Inn is immoral?" Merlyn asked, recovering from her lapse. Her dark eyebrows lifted as she stared at Mrs. Radner. "How?"

The older woman looked stunned. She faltered, searching for words. "I assumed . . ."

"Miss Forrest," Cameron began again, and his black eyes glared holes in her, "you were asked to be in by midnight."

"No, I wasn't, Mr. Thorpe. I was ordered to be in by midnight," she retorted. "I don't respond well to orders, even when they're given by exciting dark men."

"Cameron," Delle interrupted, "don't you think . . ."

46

"Keep out of this, Delle," Cameron replied curtly, as if a mere woman's comments weren't worth listening to.

Delle meekly inclined her head toward her plate, and Merlyn glowered at Delle. "Are you going to let him talk to you that way?" she burst out. "My goodness, you don't have to sit there and take orders like a family pet!"

Delle looked shocked, but her expression was nothing compared to Cameron's. He threw down his napkin as if it were a gauntlet.

"That's enough," he told Merlyn, and his voice was like deep, icy water. "That's more than enough."

"You said it, honey," Merlyn replied with a contemptuous laugh as she got to her feet, oblivious to Charlotte's glare and Lila's smothered grin. "I'd choke having to eat beside a male chauvinist like you. If you'll all excuse me, I'm going to freshen up."

She got up with a general nod in the direction of the guests and went upstairs.

"Male supremacist, sitting there like the first Caesar," she muttered, stripping off her clothes and coiling her long hair up under a borrowed shower cap as she went toward the bathroom. "And that simpering child sitting there, lapping it up!" she hissed. She turned on the water and stepped under it, quickly soaping herself and as quickly washing off the lather. She grabbed a towel and dried herself, ripped off the shower cap and shook her hair dry. Cameron had made her furious enough, but that Charlotte Radner had really set her temper on fire. Snob! How dare that woman make such assumptions about her? Of course, she had to admit that she'd deliberately begun to give the wrong impression. But she was probably worth twice as much as the Radners, and she hated being put down. If this was how poor people lived, it wasn't very pleasant. It made her think. Which was probably what her father had intended from the beginning, she thought angrily. And again she wondered if he had more than a nodding acquaintance with Cameron Thorpe. He couldn't have picked a better adversary for her if he'd spent his life searching. Then she realized she was on the wrong track. Her father would have been in search of a soul mate for her, not an adversary.

She walked back into her bedroom, sleek and elegant in her nudity, her high breasts in perfect proportion to a body that was sensuous and graceful and unconscious of its own power. And as she walked into the bedroom, Cameron Thorpe walked in the door.

Her eyes widened. So did his. They went over her like dark fingers, tracing every soft curve, every long line, with an intensity that froze her into position like a nymph caught bathing.

"Damn you!" she whispered as sanity returned. She dived for the silky blue coverlet, and jerked it around her. Her face went blood red. No man had ever seen her without her clothes, not even that jackass she'd been engaged to. There had been very little more than kissing between them, in fact, which was one thing that had led to her suspicion that her money was the attraction for Adam, not her body. Or her heart.

"How interesting," Cameron murmured, watching her reaction as she shrank against the post of the canopy over her wide bed. He closed the door behind him with a hard thud and went toward her.

She vaulted across the bed, and got behind the elegant blue wing chair, glaring at him over it. "What are you doing in here?" she demanded.

"You sound quite hysterical, Miss Forrest," he commented. He rammed his hands in his pockets and smiled slowly. The smile changed him, made him wildly sensual. The big muscles in his arms were outlined by the short-sleeved knit shirt he was wearing, and so was the muscular breadth of his chest. His slacks were close fitting, emphasizing the powerful muscles of his long legs, the slender lines of his hips and stomach. He was devastating, physically at least. And she hated herself for noticing that.

"I'm not hysterical."

"You said you were just going to freshen up. I assumed you'd had time for that by now."

He sounded reasonable, but she didn't feel reasonable. She wanted to throw things. Her fingers trembled where they held the coverlet against her breasts.

"Whatever you wanted, can't it wait until I get my clothes on?" she asked in a high-pitched tone.

"What I had in mind would work better with them off," he replied, moving toward her again.

"No hitting, if you please," she said, shoving the chair at him. "My insurance doesn't have a clause for assault and battery."

"I wouldn't hit you," he said. "I just want your full attention." He nudged the chair aside with his hip and kept coming. "Nervous, *Jane?*" he asked with a cold smile. "Isn't that what your friends call you?"

"Yes, but you don't fall into that category. I'm warning you, Mr. Thorpe, I have acquaintances who just adore suing people on my behalf!"

"So have I. Pay attention, Miss Forrest, because I don't intend to repeat this. I don't know what kind of half-baked boys you're used to, but in this house I'm the master, and what I say goes."

"Do you wear a crown, sir, and have little crests sewn on your underwear?" she asked. She backed behind the night table, using it like a shield. Part of her was nervous, but another part was wildly excited by that glitter in his eyes, the movement of his powerful body. She'd never tried to enrage a man before, but there was something about Cameron's dark, somber masculinity that intrigued her. She couldn't help but wonder what was under the mask.

He stood looking at her, his eyes narrow and intent, his head slightly cocked to one side. "Hiding?" he asked in a voice soft with menace.

She laughed again. "Just taking cover. Now, Mr. Thorpe, you knew from the beginning that I didn't just lie down and let people walk over me. I'm not any good at taking orders, and I don't intend to take them from you."

His dark eyes glittered with amusement and something deeper, more dangerous. "You're afraid of me, aren't you?" he asked, studying her posture. "Where's all that bravado you had in front of my guests?"

"It's not fear of you," she promised with a blatant

smile. "I'm just afraid that if I don't keep my distance, I might wrestle you down on the floor, that's all." Gathering her courage, she batted her eyelashes at him. "Oh, Mr. Thorpe, you're *sooooo* sexy!"

He made a rough sound. "Think so? Well, honey, you'd have to pay me."

He turned to leave, and she lost her head. "Damn you!" she breathed with glittering fury. She glared after him with eyes full of hatred.

He turned with his hand on the doorknob and studied her one last time. "You have the most beautiful body I've ever seen," he said unexpectedly. "Are you a virgin?"

She held the coverlet tighter. "Guessing?"

His eyes wandered over her. "Miss Forrest, an experienced woman doesn't run for cover at the first sign of male interest. Just for future reference."

She tossed her hair. "I don't need instructions. Least of all from someone who sleeps in a bed full of ice cubes."

His eyebrows arched. "Do you think I do?" He put his hands in his pockets and studied her curiously.

"I'll give you my character analysis of you on the day I leave here," she promised.

He looked her over again, with calculating eyes. "Delle and her mother left a few minutes ago, by the way, and I'm on my way out now," he said with a cool smile. "Thanks to you, I had some explaining to do. They seem to feel that you're here for my benefit, not my mother's. I set them straight." He lifted his square jaw and pursed his lips. "There's just one thing you'd better keep in mind. In case you don't know it, I pay the bills. Including my mother's. That makes me your real boss, and if you want trouble, put me in the same position twice."

"You can count on my cooperation, sir," she said huskily, and grinned.

"I thought you'd see it my way. I'm glad we had this little talk, Jane," he added with a superior smile. "Just dig up bodies for my mother, and you and I will get along fine."

"I'll do my very best," she promised. An impish smile touched her full lips. "But just hold your breath until I lay my heart at your feet again."

Amazingly, he laughed. And it was genuine, for once. "Damned brat," he muttered as he jerked open the door. "Too bad we're from such different worlds, Jane Eyre," he said with a curt laugh. "I think I could have made you lay more than your heart at my feet a few years back."

She blinked. "A few years back?"

"Before I learned what devious, twisted minds you women have. Before Amanda's mother taught me how beautifully deceit can be clothed." He rammed his hands in his pockets and stared at her. "I don't have any inclination to lose my heart again."

"Delle would be crushed to hear you say that," Merlyn replied.

"Delle will make a good wife," he returned. "She's young and impressionable and easily led. She dresses beautifully and she knows how to be a good hostess. The perfect businessman's wife. Our marriage will be a very profitable merger."

"Mama comes with her," she reminded him. "And she isn't easily led."

"Mama is a barracuda. But I'm a shark."

She wouldn't have touched that line with a cattle prod.

His eyes wandered down the coverlet and back up again, and there was something in them that frightened Merlyn more than his earlier anger.

"I don't like domineering men," she said.

"I wasn't aware that your job required you to like me."

She laughed. "Praise the Lord."

His head tilted and he smiled slowly. "You're full of fire, Miss Forrest," he murmured. "Like a firecracker. I'd forgotten how exciting it could be. . . ." As if the observation angered him, his smile vanished and the glitter was back in his eyes. "Stop prodding me, for your own good. I make a bad enemy. And since you apparently don't work for the fun of it, I'd hate to see you kicked out the door over an insignificant disagreement."

He inclined his head like a conquering general and went out, leaving her puzzled, excited, and on edge. She had underestimated him. But it was a mistake she wouldn't make again.

"They're gone, Merlyn," Amanda whispered as Merlyn came downstairs to find the little girl waiting for her. Amanda grinned. "Now we can get back to normal."

"Don't you like Miss Radner?" Merlyn asked gently.

Amanda glowered. "She doesn't like me," she muttered. "She looks at me as if she feels sorry for me. Just you wait, someday I'll be just as elegant as she is, and I'll feel sorry for her, on account of she'll be old and ugly!"

Merlyn laughed, tugging the young girl against her. "You're pretty enough to suit me, Miss Thorpe. And all you need is a haircut, a big smile, and some confidence to make you into a raving beauty."

Amanda stopped and looked up at her, wide-eyed. "Do you really think so?"

"Yes, I do."

"Could you cut my hair?"

Merlyn pursed her lips. "When I get through working, I'll ask your father if I can take you into town to a beauty shop. Okay?"

"I'll ask him, when he comes back next weekend. He said he was going to," Amanda volunteered. She blushed. "He doesn't like women, mostly, except for Miss Radner. But he likes me."

"Yes, darling, I'm sure he does. I like you, too."

Amanda smiled. "You're not bad, for a grown-up. You're sort of different."

Yes, I'm that, Merlyn thought mischievously. Very different from the sort of grown-up you're used to. Like Cameron Thorpe. She wanted to have nothing to do with a man who could contemplate marriage to a woman just because she suited his lifestyle. She wondered if he really thought his Delle was such a prize. Despite her beauty, she struck Merlyn as a passionless woman, appealing to look at, but that was all. That was his business, though. Hers was going to be keeping out of his way. She wouldn't heel on command for any overbearing stuffed shirt, but on the other hand she didn't want to have to go home and admit defeat. Her father was already sure she couldn't win this bet; she wasn't going to prove him right. No, she'd just have to depend on her sense of humor to keep Cameron Thorpe at bay. Besides, there was always the possibility that he'd stay away from the lake house for the duration of her month's employment.

Cameron's absence was a blessing. For the rest of the week, the lake was delightfully peaceful. Merlyn took Amanda into town, with her grandmother's permission—Lila had said the child's hair was none of Cameron's business—and had her hair cut. As an afterthought, she bought her a new dress, too—a lovely, frilly thing in blue that suited the young girl.

"You shouldn't spend your money on me," Amanda protested. "You don't make a lot. I heard Grandmother arguing about it with my father. He said . . ." She stopped, flushing.

"He said what?" Merlyn probed softly.

"Well, it was something mean." She glanced up apprehensively. "He said you weren't worth what you were getting paid and that Grandmother ought to get someone else. But Grandmama stuck up for you," she continued quickly. "She said if he fired you, he could go back to Charleston and stay there. She's real mad about him bringing Delle and Mrs. Radner here. She says Daddy only wants to marry Delle on account of she's rich."

In other words, Lila was blackmailing him. Merlyn felt miserable for the rest of the day about his opinion of her. It shouldn't have been so hurtful, but it was.

"I ought to resign," she told Lila finally, as they sat

together at the kitchen table and had coffee after Amanda had gone to bed. "Amanda told me about the argument you had with your son."

Lila grinned. "Did she? Don't worry about Cam, I can handle him."

"I don't want to cause trouble." Merlyn stared into her black coffee. "He antagonizes me, though. Sometimes I can't help it. But I'll do my best to be pleasant to him, if it will keep the peace."

"But I don't want you to be pleasant to him," Lila said surprisingly, with a twinkle in her eyes. "He was angry when he left here. Angrier than I've seen him in years. It was a pleasant change from his usual indifference. You've shaken him, Merlyn. Keep it up."

"That would be risky," Merlyn murmured with a delicate shudder, remembering his threat.

"I'll protect you," Lila promised. She searched Merlyn's eyes. "Merlyn, did you feel the undercurrents, when the Radners were here?"

Merlyn shifted restlessly. "It's really none of my affair."

"Delle's father has a very profitable investment corporation. She'll inherit it. Cam has decided, in a coldblooded way, that she'll make him a good wife." She sighed miserably. "You see, dear, my husband left us deeply in debt. He borrowed too much, and he had friends who were too kind to refuse him credit. When he died, there were insurmountable bills. We even sold the family estate, which our ancestors built over a hundred years ago, to defray the debt. But it still wasn't enough. Cam is slowly getting us back on our feet, and what I make with my writing helps." She laughed softly. "I won't deny that having money in the family again would be a tremendous boost to our small assets, but I don't want Cam to ruin his whole life just to get out of debt."

Merlyn studied her hands. "He doesn't seem the kind of man who'd marry solely for money," she murmured, looking up into Lila's surprised face.

"It isn't just that," Lila returned. "You're very perceptive, Merlyn. No, it isn't only money. He wants a home and a mother for Amanda. He wants permanence." She shrugged. "He's rather rootless right now. He lives and works in Charleston, but he's always out looking for new investors. He's spent a lot of time in Atlanta lately, courting the head of a new corporation that's locating back home. Beating out the competition way ahead of time," she explained with a grin.

"Why Delle?" Merlyn asked with genuine curiosity.

Lila grimaced. "He met her at a party, liked her poise, and set out to court her. I don't know what he sees in her. She's so fussy about her hair and clothes that I don't imagine he even gets to touch her, and she's years too young for him. But," she sighed, "he doesn't listen to me anymore."

During the next three days they worked at a comfortable, steady pace, while Amanda fished and played on the lake.

"I love this," Merlyn said on Friday, as she lounged on the dock with her legs hanging off the side and a fishing pole in her hand. She was wearing a blue tube top, cut-offs that showed her tanned, slender legs to their best advantage, and a floppy hat on her head.

"What, fishing?" Lila asked as she sunbathed nearby. It was the first real break they'd taken, and they felt they both deserved it. They'd gotten through a tremendous amount of work.

"Fishing. Working. Being here on the lake." Merlyn shifted her pole experimentally to make sure the bait was still on the hook, and tossed it back in. "I hadn't realized how pleasant it could be."

"Why do you think I come here to work?" Lila laughed. "Of course, I'm usually alone with Tilly and Amanda. Cameron doesn't often come here."

With the pole in hand, Merlyn leaned back against the warm boards, hoping Cameron would indeed stay away. The sun felt good, and the only sounds were of birds and crickets and the wind. She felt the warm breeze over her face and sighed with pure delight.

The sudden tug on the line caught her unawares, and she felt the fishing pole being dragged out of her fingers. "Oh, no, you don't, you sneaky fish!"

She made a grab for the pole, but it was dragged off the pier, obviously being tugged away by something with scales and a smug look on its fishy face.

Impulsively, she jumped into the lake after it, swimming smoothly toward the pole with the graceful style she'd been taught in her youth. She grabbed the pole and dog-paddled toward shore with it firmly under one arm.

"You got it, Merlyn!" Amanda squealed, jumping up and down. "You got it!"

Lila was grinning, too, clapping her hands in amusement.

"Stupid fish," Merlyn muttered as she got to the bank and collapsed on it. The water had been cold, but she hadn't even noticed. The pole was still being tugged, so she dragged herself to her feet and put all her remaining strength into fighting whatever was on the end of the line.

"Try to get away from me, will you?" she muttered. She was no novice at pulling in fighting fish. She frequently went deep-sea fishing with her father in the Gulf of Mexico. Huffing and puffing, she matched pull with tug, until with one quick, sharp jerk, she flipped the fish out of the water . . . and right into Cameron Thorpe's face as he walked toward her down the slight hill.

4

~~∞∞∞∞∞∞∞∞∞~~

She heard a harsh curse as she turned around.

"Oops," she said, glancing toward Lila and Amanda, who were in tears, they were laughing so hard.

"Why the hell did you do that?" Cameron growled, dabbing with his handkerchief at the expensive tan vested suit he was wearing. "My God, this suit cost a small fortune, and now it smells like a bad seafood restaurant."

Merlyn moved closer and picked up her wriggling fish, which lay in the dirt next to Cameron's expensive shoes. She held it up with a sigh. It was a carp, not even a terribly big one. And it was making pitiful little noises. With a wistful glance, she heaved it back into the lake.

"You got it all dirty," she said, glowering at

Cameron. "And it will probably lose every friend it's got when they get a good whiff of it."

He stared at her with wide, uncomprehending eyes.

"Why do you wear that horrible stuff, anyway?" she asked. "British Sterling is so much more impressive, and it doesn't smell like a dead animal."

One corner of his mouth lifted, as if he were tempted to smile. His dark eyes wandered down to her wet tube top and lingered on the outline of her high breasts. Something stirred in his face, and she knew that he was remembering how she looked without her clothes. She might as well be topless; the top was so thin that everything showed. Involuntarily, her arms crossed over it and she took a step backward.

"Are you cold?" he asked quietly. His eyes moved back up to hers, and it was like getting an electric shock. "Or do I excite you, Miss Forrest?"

She knew exactly what he meant, and her face flushed. "Now, now, Mr. Rochester," she murmured, "let's not get personal."

One corner of that hard mouth curled up. "Are you sure you don't want to? You might be enough to tempt me, after all."

She glared at him. "I need to change."

"Not on my account," he murmured for her ears alone as the others came toward them. "You have exquisite breasts."

She clenched her fingers and caught her breath, feeling murderous urges. Her glittering green eyes met his at point-blank range, and he gave a soft, predatory laugh.

Hard, she'd called him. Cold and stiff and as

romantic as a crab. And now here he was throwing her off balance, when it should have been the reverse. She turned away.

"How very odd—that Merlyn goes fishing and you get the catch," Lila murmured to her son, looking amused.

"It all depends on what you're fishing for, I suppose," he replied.

"All I've caught is a chill." Merlyn laughed nervously. "I'd better put on something dry."

"Yes, dear, we don't want you getting sick."

"I'll come and help," Amanda volunteered, and followed Merlyn into the house.

Cameron was rapidly becoming an unknown quantity. He watched Merlyn blatantly over the supper table, and it was all she could do to eat.

"Will Delle and her mother be back any time soon?" Lila asked her son.

He glanced at her, toying with his wineglass. "Next weekend. I'm giving a party, by the way. We'll want a caterer and a band."

"A party," Lila repeated enthusiastically. "How lovely."

"You'll come, of course, Miss Forrest," he added with a dark, intent stare. "We wouldn't want you to feel left out."

"But I'm only a humble employee, sir," she said, holding on to her sense of humor. He was up to something, but she wasn't going to give him any openings. "And perfectly content to sit among the cinders."

"It will be formal," he continued, with a pointed

glance at the outfit she was wearing. "And something conservative, please," he added in a long-suffering tone.

"Like that uniform you wear?" she returned sweetly, noting the suit he'd changed into.

He frowned. "What?"

"Gray suit, white shirt, gray tie," she replied. "It's always the same shirt, always a tie the same color as the suit—always the same suit in fascinating shades of gray or brown or blue. Don't you like plaids and stripes and florals, Mr. Thorpe?"

"I'm not a woman," he returned.

She sighed, leaned her chin dreamily on her clasped hands, and stared at him. "No, sir, you sure aren't," she murmured huskily.

His dark eyes narrowed. "You'll have to wear an evening gown, or at least a cocktail dress," he continued.

She shrugged. "In that case," she replied, "I suppose I'll have to go shopping. I didn't come prepared for a ball."

"There's a lovely little shop in the mall," Lila told her.

"Yes, I saw it," Merlyn sighed. "They had some pretty gowns."

"You can have an advance on your salary, if you need it," Cameron said pleasantly.

She glared at him. "How odd. I had the feeling that you didn't think I was worth the salary I was already getting?"

One dark eyebrow lifted. "I wonder what made you say that?" he countered, glancing in Lila's direction.

Merlyn could have gone through the floor. No, she

couldn't let Lila take the blame. "I was outside the door, actually," she lied smoothly.

"Eavesdropping?" he muttered.

"Well, I thought you might be about to confess undying love for me," Merlyn said outrageously. "And I know that you're basically a shy man . . ."

Lila burst out laughing, and Amanda looked delighted.

Cameron only stared at her. His dark, graceful fingers seemed to caress the wineglass. "Are you propositioning me, Miss Forrest?" he asked pleasantly.

The counterattack was unexpected. Merlyn fought to keep from overreacting. "Why, no, sir," she said fervently. "I'm an old-fashioned girl, you see, and what I had in mind was that you would seek my hand in—do I dare mention it—marriage."

He chuckled softly, amusedly. "Touché."

Merlyn smiled at him over her coffee. It was becoming a contest between them, to see who could score off the other first. The cold, hard man of her first meeting was slowly but surely coming out of his shell. But at what cost to Merlyn's shredded nerves!

"I'm sorry to disappoint you," he told Merlyn suavely, "but you're not my type."

"Too much woman for you, hmmm?" She grinned.

He burst out laughing. "Too little."

That rankled, but she wouldn't let it show. She raised her coffee cup in a mock salute and drained it. "I'll be kind and let that barb pass me by."

"How is the research progressing?" he asked his mother.

"Very well, indeed. We've settled on a pattern for a character and a period of time for the setting."

"Which?" he asked.

"Early Tudor," Merlyn replied.

"Henry Tudor?" he asked with an arched brow. "You needn't look so shocked, Miss Forrest, I minored in history."

"Your period?"

"Ancient Greece."

She sighed. "Pericles . . . Herodotus . . . Socrates . . . Plato . . ."

"Ah, a student."

"An eternal student," she agreed. "I enjoyed the ruins, especially the site of Troy. You read about Heinrich Schliemann, of course? Amazing, how he used the ancient texts to . . ."

"You enjoyed the ruins?" He pounced on that, his eyes emphasizing his obvious contention that she couldn't afford a raft to float to Greece on.

"In the books I borrowed from the library, of course," she said quickly. "No, Mr. Thorpe, I could hardly afford a leisurely cruise to the Mediterranean, as you've reminded me so often."

"Stop baiting me," he said. "What did you most enjoy studying?"

"The kings of England. The royal family fascinates me," she confessed. "And the founding of the Tudor line was a particularly romantic period."

"Yes, romance does seem to play an important part in your life," he observed with a curt laugh. "How many times have you read *Jane Eyre?*"

"A dozen," she replied. "It's a lovely book. And you did rather appear out of the dark looking like Edward Rochester that night."

"I wasn't riding a horse, and I didn't have a dog at my heels," he reminded her.

"Mere details."

"Well, what character are you doing?" he asked Lila, going back to his original subject.

"A character loosely based on Jasper Tudor," she told him.

"Can you get enough information?"

"Merlyn already has," Lila told him. "She's a wonder. I've never seen the like of the books she brought with her."

"Rob a bank?" he asked Merlyn pleasantly. "Or are they library books?"

"They were presents," she mumbled. "From my father."

Which was true. And they had cost a mint—some of them were out-of-print editions. She'd have to keep them out of his sight, or he might start making embarrassing connections.

After that, the conversation turned to politics, and Merlyn found herself caught up in it. It was a subject she knew a bit about, having helped friends of her father campaign from time to time. Cameron had a sharp, quick mind and inevitably they argued on issues. But he made valid points, and she enjoyed the heated exchanges. Lila only watched, a secretive smile playing around her lips.

"I have to confess, I'd forgotten what a challenge an educated mind could be," Cameron said eventually, his eyes thoughtful as they studied Merlyn.

"Delle isn't college educated?" Lila asked.

He glared at his mother. "Delle's mind is quite sharp enough to suit me," he said.

"But Merlyn can fish," Amanda said shyly, joining the conversation for the first time.

Cameron glanced at his daughter. "So she can," he said. Amazingly, he smiled. "Were you fishing, too?"

"Yes, Daddy."

He glanced at Merlyn, then back at his daughter. "I thought you didn't like to handle the worms, Amanda."

"Merlyn did it for me," the child volunteered smugly.

"Barbaric," Cameron commented.

"It is not barbaric," Merlyn told him with a flash of green eyes. "The worms obviously had nothing left to live for. I was simply helping them into the next world."

"And the fish?"

"Same difference," she returned. "The whole thing is quite humane, you see."

"What a bright idea," Lila said. "I've wondered for years how to rationalize that cruel sport."

"Mother would spare every wild creature on earth if she had her way," Cameron said darkly. "She belongs to a dozen societies for the preservation of animals that no one ever heard of."

"You think conservation is an unworthy cause, Mr. Thorpe?" Merlyn asked. She leaned her chin on her hands and glared at him. "If there are no more trees, there won't be any more oxygen. They take in carbon dioxide and return oxygen into the atmosphere. If we don't preserve the wildlife habitats, there won't be wildlife. If we kill off the predators, we'll be overrun with rodents. If we let the seas die, every single living thing goes the way of them.

Do, please, give me your views on the joys of pollution.''

"My God, another one," he groaned.

"Merlyn! I'm delighted!" Lila said enthusiastically. "You must attend the next meeting of the conservation society with me."

"I already belong to a dozen," she replied, glaring across the table at Cameron. "And I've marched in rallies and written nasty letters, and once I organized a fund-raiser to help stop the spraying of a potentially dangerous insecticide."

"A radical," Cameron accused. "A card-carrying radical."

"You bet," she replied. "And proud of it."

"You'd probably like to make all the wild off limits to man. But you do enjoy your creature comforts, don't you?" he persisted. "The lipstick you're wearing has a petroleum base. So, probably, does that polyester and cotton top. Petroleum comes from off-shore drilling, which often causes pollution. The food you're eating was cooked on an electric stove, and electricity comes from the harnessing and development of rivers. The chair you're sitting on is made of wood, which means that a tree died to provide you with it. Now look smug."

Merlyn tossed down her napkin and measured the distance between his head and her coffee cup.

He got to his feet with a mocking bow. "That's why I don't contribute to every preservation society that asks for a donation. Good evening."

She slammed the table with her hand and let out an angry breath. "He's incorrigible!" she told the coffee cup.

Lila laughed. "Yes. But despite his apparent opposition to environmental causes, he contributes heavily to the Cousteau Society and Greenpeace, among others," she confided. "I happened to see the check stubs. He'd hidden them in the safe."

"Daddy keeps his causes to himself," Amanda added. "He was just leading you along, Merlyn. He's a fanatic, too."

The thought kept Merlyn awake half the night. Cameron was turning out to be so different from what she'd assumed. He was almost frighteningly intelligent. He was involved and he cared. But he kept all that hidden behind a mask of indifferent hauteur, which apparently no one but family was allowed close enough to penetrate. She doubted if Delle had ever been privileged to see the real man.

And yet he was contemplating marriage with the young woman. A merger, he'd said. Two companies. Nothing more. But he was obviously a passionate man. Did he desire Delle? Did he care for her? Merlyn seriously doubted it. But he'd as much as admitted that she herself could attract him that way. She flushed at the memory of his deep voice drawling it. He was dangerous, all right, and she had no intention of getting involved with him. But, physically, he made her tingle and burn. And she didn't like that at all. She was tempted to give up the job and go home. But that wouldn't be fair to Lila. And she couldn't just let her father win. She sighed. Well, she'd just avoid Cameron. That would be the best way to cope.

* * *

On Monday Cameron went back to Charleston, and the women went back to work. By the end of the week, Merlyn got to read the first few chapters of Lila's book as the writing started in earnest. She was fascinated by the amount of work the elderly woman could get through in a day, by the number of pages she produced.

"Ah, but it's not as if I'm doing it by myself," Lila said when they set to work. The morning was overcast so they were sitting in the library. "I just sit at the computer and inspiration comes. I can't really take credit for what I do."

Merlyn grinned at her. "It must be wonderful."

"It's a gift. One I never take for granted," Lila confided. She turned on the computer and sighed. "I don't know how in the world I managed with that old electric typewriter. It seems utterly archaic compared with this computer."

"Dad makes those," Merlyn blurted out and instantly regretted it.

"Computers?" Lila asked.

"The, uh, kit form, I meant."

"Oh," Lila said with a grin. "I couldn't do that to save my life. He must be very smart."

"He's that," Merlyn agreed. Several million dollars in the bank attested to her father's brilliance in computers and components.

"Well, what do you think?" Lila asked, nodding toward the manuscript in Merlyn's lap.

"It's marvelous," Merlyn said sincerely. "I love it! I'm so proud to have even a little part in the project."

"You've got quite a large part, actually," the older

woman said with a laugh. "I don't think I'd have dared undertake it without you."

"Undertake?" Cameron asked as he joined them, with Amanda at his side. "An odd choice of words, isn't it, Mother?"

He was wearing white that morning. White slacks and a white and red patterned shirt. He looked dark and dangerous and good enough to eat, and something in Merlyn reacted wildly to his presence, even though she'd heard his car drive up the night before. It was Saturday morning, but it felt like the beginning of a new lifetime, and she tingled all over just from looking at him. She deliberately avoided his eyes.

Lila smiled. "You look nice this morning, Cam."

"The Radners come today, had you forgotten?"

I was trying to, Merlyn thought wickedly.

"No, dear, of course not," Lila said. "Everything's quite organized for tonight. Merlyn contacted the band for me. It seems that she knows one of the members."

Those dark, intent eyes fixed on her. "Does she?"

It was a challenge. She peeked up at him. "Oh, yes," she told him. "He's a friend of long standing."

It was her friend Dick Langley, the race car driver. She'd sworn him to secrecy about her true identity when she called him. Dick had been glad to oblige. In his spare time he sat in with a local band and played drums. Just for fun. God knew, he had enough money to do whatever he liked. Besides, he liked to put one over on people. And Merlyn's masquerade had piqued his interest.

"What does your friend play?" Cameron asked.

"Drums," she told him. "And he's very good."

"A passionate instrument," he replied casually. Too casually.

"He's a passionate man," she murmured with a secretive smile.

"I can't wait to meet him," Lila said. "He sounds quite interesting."

"He'll wind up in a book if he is," Cameron muttered.

"He will not," Lila grumbled. "I've told you a hundred times that I don't put real people in books. It would be suicide. I'd be sued to the back teeth."

"Sorry, Mother," he said with a dry smile. "I forgot."

"No, you didn't," Lila countered, rising. "You simply like to start fights, Cam. It's a bad habit you've fallen into."

"I'm trying to break it," he assured her, but the glance he gave Merlyn was far from reassuring. She kept out of his way the rest of the day.

Dick Langley delivered her gown—a devastating green velvet—that evening. It was a designer dress that she'd had him bring from her father's house. He handed her the box as he came in with the band.

"One masquerade gown, intact, despite the fact that it's pouring out there," he said. He was almost as tall as Cameron, but blond and blue-eyed and overdosed with charm. He was using it now, trying—as he had for years—to catch Merlyn's eye.

"Thanks for bringing it. And for bringing the group," she added. "Only the best, you know."

"What are you up to, lady?" he asked, moving aside as the other four members of the band filed in, along with the caterers.

"Something sinful," she whispered, smiling.

He bent and brushed his mouth lazily over hers, a teasing, undemanding caress that was pleasant and nothing more. "After the gig's over, let's discuss sinful things together."

"We'll see," she murmured demurely.

"Devil woman," he whispered. He winked and turned away toward the large living room, which had been cleared for dancing.

"An old lover?" Cameron asked from behind her, his eyes glittering as he stared after Dick. He was wearing dark evening clothes, and he smelled of a delicious manly fragrance. Her earlier criticism of his cologne had been pure fabrication.

"An old friend," she countered, clutching her box.

His eyes narrowed on it. "He bought you a dress?" he growled. "For God's sake . . . !"

The assumption made her furious. "So what if he bought me a dress?" she challenged. "What business is it of yours?"

He glowered down at her. "You're an employee here."

"Not a slave, Mr. Rochester—would you keep that in mind?" she shot back. "If you want me to leave, say so."

He looked as if he was about to, when Delle came marching in just ahead of her mother. They were elegantly dressed, Delle in a peach-colored silk dress that reached to the floor and hugged her ample bosom. Mrs. Radner looked stern and formal, as usual, in a lacy black gown with a high Victorian neckline.

"Not coming to the dance, Miss Forrest?" Mrs. Radner asked coolly, staring at Merlyn's jeans and shirt.

"As a matter of fact, I am," Merlyn replied sweetly, clutching her box. "My dress just arrived. If you'll excuse me?"

"Cameron, you've hardly said two words to me since we got here," Delle was complaining as Merlyn scurried upstairs. "Can't you spare just five minutes?"

Merlyn almost felt sorry for the girl. She was so infatuated, and Cameron, damn him, was treating her like a piece of candy he wasn't sure he wanted. Men, she thought angrily, were all alike.

She passed Lila on the way to her room. The older woman was wearing white, a beautiful gown that, in its simplicity, outshone the Radners' outfits.

"Gorgeous," Merlyn told her. "Halston, isn't it?"

Lila looked shocked. "Why, yes."

"I thought so. Such fluid lines. Well, I'll get my gown on and see you later." She smiled and walked into her room. Oops, she thought as she closed the door. She'd almost given herself away again. A penniless scholar wouldn't have known a Halston gown on sight. But Merlyn, who'd been fortunate enough to have her trousseau done by Halston, knew the designs well. Her eyes clouded. She'd had such high hopes for Adam and herself. It had been a devastating blow, to find that he hadn't wanted her—physically or any other way.

She dressed angrily, hating Adam, hating herself for being so blind. And now she was beginning to daydream about that horrible Cameron. Well, she'd just have to stop it. This was a job that would soon be over. Nothing more.

She tugged on her gown and its matching shoes and fixed her hair in a high, elegant coiffure. She used more makeup than usual, emphasizing her thick, long lashes, her full mouth and her high cheekbones. She fastened her mother's pearls around her throat, put on the matching earrings and stared at herself in the mirror. Well, Miss Radner, she thought wickedly, top that.

"Wow," came a soft little voice from the doorway.

She turned to Amanda, smiling at the awe on the young girl's face. Merlyn knew she looked good in the designer gown. It was a long sheath of dark green velvet with a strapless bodice composed of pleated satin only a shade lighter than the velvet. It was an altogether bewitching dress, and the pearls set it off beautifully.

"Are you really Merlyn?" Amanda asked. "You sure do look different."

Merlyn went forward to kiss the girl warmly. "You make me feel like a fairy princess. I just hope my pumpkin doesn't vanish."

"Not before midnight, anyway." Amanda giggled. "Good night. Have fun."

"I hope to. Sleep well, darling."

She left Amanda at her own room and continued down the stairs. The band had just started playing, and the tune was one Dick had chosen deliberately. It dated back to their high school days, a lazy tune that was pure seduction.

She paused in the doorway to the living room.

Cameron spotted her instantly and stopped dead in the middle of the dance floor with Delle in his arms.

Merlyn nodded at them and continued to the buffet table where Lila was busily filling a plate.

"Darling!" she said as Merlyn came up beside her. "That gown! Tracy Mills, isn't it?"

Merlyn laughed softly. "Yes. Sharp eyes."

"Even if they are old," Lila murmured. "What a knockout you are. And so poised. Merlyn, you're deceiving us or I'm a has-been."

"Deceiving you?" She was breathless.

"You're not what you appear to be," the older woman clarified. Her sharp eyes narrowed.

"The gown is borrowed," Merlyn whispered, pretending for all she was worth. "I have a friend with clout, if you know what I mean."

Lila glanced sideways toward the band.

"Exactly." Merlyn grinned. "He has a sister just my size," she confided. Well, it was sort of the truth. Except that Dick's sister was still in high school and wore a size 18 dress.

"Oh," Lila said and smiled. "Well, you look lovely."

Cameron and Delle joined them. "My, my, what a pretty dress," Delle said, staring at it.

"Thank you," Merlyn said graciously.

"And the pearls—they look so real! Isn't it amazing what they can do with costume jewelry these days," Delle continued, not even meaning to be malicious.

Merlyn lifted an eyebrow and smiled. "Yes, isn't it?" she replied, looking pointedly at Delle's gaudy sapphire necklace. "Paste?"

Delle flushed wildly. "Well . . . I mean, you do

realize that the original is quite too expensive to wear in public!"

"Oh, I'm sure it is," Merlyn said with a cool smile. "By the way, dear, these pearls are quite real. They've been in my family for three generations, and if you'll take a close look, you'll see that they're perfectly matched."

Delle looked flustered. Merlyn was amazed at her own temerity. Usually she just let snobs be snobs, but the girl had hit a nerve. There was no real reason for her to dislike Delle, but she did. She disliked her almost as much as she felt sorry for her.

"Would you like to dance, Miss Forrest?" Cameron asked with a cold smile. He took her hand before she could protest and nodded at a stunned Delle as he pulled Merlyn onto the dance floor.

"You're pushing your luck," he said bluntly, glaring down at her. "Stop chewing on Delle, or I'll try my teeth on you."

"How protective, Mr. Thorpe," she drawled sweetly. "Lucky Delle."

"Those pearls *are* real, aren't they?" he asked, staring at them. "Were they really your grandmother's?"

"Yes, they were. The one good piece of jewelry I possess, and I dislike having them laughed at by little girls with no manners," she said curtly.

His eyebrow went up. "Such hauteur for a working girl," he murmured.

"Even working girls have pride, Mr. Thorpe," she returned, her eyes glittering at him.

He pulled her closer, bringing her breasts against

77

the front of his dark jacket. He glanced down, peeking past the satin to the warm, white slopes of her breasts. "What an enchanting gown," he murmured. "Just made to tempt a man's eyes. Is that why you chose it?"

She hadn't honestly contemplated this complication. She tried to draw back, but he wouldn't let her.

"Stay where you are," he said quietly. "You look good enough to eat."

"Thank you," she muttered, glaring up at him.

His hand spread out against her bare back, and she felt fire where his hard fingers touched and probed. "Silk," he murmured. "Silk and satin and velvet. A dangerous combination."

"Delle is staring at us. And I'm very hungry," she returned.

"Let Delle stare. You ate lunch."

"I'm hungry again."

"A woman of large appetite," he said, searching her eyes. "I have a large one of my own, Merlyn."

Her face flamed and her eyes flashed. She stopped dancing. "If you're going to make crude innuendoes . . ."

"I'll reform, if I must," he murmured dryly, drawing her back into the slow rhythm.

"Poor little thing," she said, glancing past him to Delle, who looked very young and lost and frightened.

"Who, Delle?" He laughed. "Here comes Mama. She won't be lost for long."

Merlyn noticed the older woman entering the room. Mrs. Radner's sharp blue eyes picked out Cameron, widened when she saw Merlyn, and glittered when they found Delle all alone. She lifted her head like a spirited thoroughbred and made her way to the buffet table.

"She reminds me vaguely of a race horse," Merlyn said absently. "One with its ears back."

He chuckled deeply and pulled her hard against him as he executed a graceful turn. "You remind me of a nervous filly," he said, bending so that his breath brushed her ear. "Your body feels like a board. Why don't you relax?"

"It would be suicide," she said without thinking.

"Would it?"

5

The tone of his voice was like velvet, and it made her feel liquid in his big arms. His hand pressed harder against her back. "Would it, Merlyn?" he repeated softly.

"Yes," she whispered, peeking up at him through her dark lashes.

She'd expected the coquetry to make him smile, but he didn't. If anything he looked more formidable than the night they'd met. He held her tight as he whirled her around, and she couldn't seem to break the hypnotism of his gaze.

"You smell of gardenias," he said quietly, "and I could get drunk on the feel of your skin. Your name suits you. Merlyn. Magic."

She felt hot all over. With an effort, she looked away from him. Things were getting out of hand. "Could we stop?" she asked in a high-pitched little voice. "Delle must want to dance with you, she's glaring at us."

"Delle can wait," he murmured.

The waltz ended abruptly, but he didn't let go, and the band immediately began a lazy, bluesy tune that invited closer contact.

"Please, I don't want to," she said softly.

He only shook his head, folding her back into his arms. He moved lightly, gracefully, amid the throng, while Delle and her mother looked daggers at them. There was going to be trouble there, Merlyn thought with resignation.

"Stop worrying," he said, bending closer. "We're only dancing."

But it didn't feel like only dancing, and his big, warm hand on her bare back was doing the most fascinating things to her pulse rate. She was leaning against his broad chest with no idea of how she got there, and he was holding her close enough that her thighs brushed his when they moved.

Merlyn wasn't a child. She'd been engaged, and although she hadn't experienced it herself, she knew how potent a man's lovemaking could be. But what Cameron Thorpe was doing to her had never happened before, certainly not with Adam. He was making her tremble with every touch of his body. She could feel its warmth all the way up and down her own. She could smell the clean, spicy scent of his skin and sense the growing hunger in him.

It shouldn't be like this, she told herself. I shouldn't be reacting to him this way. But even as she began the silent lecture, his hand dropped down to her waist and pressed her closer, and she trembled even more.

He stiffened as he felt it. His hand froze and then pressed urgently. His dark head bent so that his breath was at her ear as the couples dancing around them nudged them even closer.

"You're potent, Jane Eyre," he growled in her ear. "Can you feel what you're doing to me?"

She could and it was embarrassing. She shifted quickly, smoothly, and wouldn't look at him. "Delle is watching," she threatened, although she couldn't see the woman. There was pure panic in her voice, and he recognized it.

"There's nothing to be afraid of," he whispered deeply, his voice as dark as his hair, as sensuous as his muscular body close to hers. "Don't start looking for exits."

His fingers moved slowly along her spine, exciting, enticing, and she reached around her to try to stop them. It was just the opening he wanted. He caught her wrist and, using it as a lever, arched her body into the contours of his.

Her eyes met his searching gaze, and the people around them vanished. The world narrowed to his dark, broad face and the intense hunger she read in his eyes.

"Your heart is beating like a wild thing," he whispered huskily. His chest rose and fell heavily.

"Let me go, Cameron," she whispered back, shaking.

"You make my name sound like a moan," he breathed, turning suddenly so that she was intimately pressed to him for an instant. "I could make you moan, Merlyn. I know all the tricks, all the ways."

That was what she was afraid of. She wanted to pull

free and run, but he was like a narcotic. Her eyes melted into his, and she wanted nothing more at that moment than a room where they could be alone. She wanted to know the possession of that hard, chiseled mouth.

His nostrils flared as he caught her gazing at his lips, and he seemed to take the thought out of her mind. "I want that, too," he said in a rough whisper. "Your mouth and mine, tasting, hurting . . . God, let's get out of here!"

He stopped dancing with a hard jerk, oblivious to the other couples, and pushed her ahead of him in the general direction of the punch bowl. She felt alive as she never had before in her life. Her mind tried to stop her, but her body wanted him. She went where he guided her, past the punch bowl, through the milling guests and into the hall toward the study. But there were people there, too. He held her hand tightly in his, his eyes flashing wildly, his body looking as taut as her own felt. Finally, his eyes turned to the big hall closet and he tugged her hand.

He opened the door while the hall was temporarily clear and put her inside, turning on the light as he closed the door firmly behind them.

"Now," he murmured gruffly, reaching for her. He pulled her against him, unfastening his jacket and vest with an impatient hand before he pushed her arms under them, and around his broad chest. "Now, Merlyn," he whispered. "I've gone hungry for you long enough."

Her lips parted even as his mouth touched them. It was just as she'd imagined it would be. He tasted of brandy and smoke, and his mouth was every bit as hard as it looked. It did wildly sensuous things to hers, teasing and lifting, teasing and brushing, until she ached for completion. His hands smoothed over the bareness of her back above the dress, his fingers caressing.

"Harder," she whispered huskily, her voice faintly pleading.

His breath drew in sharply. "How hard?" he breathed back, biting her mouth. "Like that?"

"No," she moaned, stretching on her tiptoes. "No, like this . . . !"

Her mouth opened, coaxing his, inciting it, and her tongue traced the broad, hard line of his lips in ways she'd never liked with other men. But with him it was sweeter than wine, hotter than fire. Her kiss dragged a moan from his throat, and caused his hands to move low on her hips and grind them into his.

"Oh!" she burst out.

He lifted his head to look down at her. His eyes were blazing, and his jaw was taut and rigid. The eyes he looked into were softer than the velvet of her dress, half-closed, lazy with ardor. "Enough?" he asked mockingly.

She made a soft little movement with her head, and her hands slid around him, to his chest, to the buttons of his shirt. Her eyes opened as they searched his.

"Go ahead," he said quietly. "Just don't excite me too much. The closet isn't the place for what we're building up to."

She realized that, of course she did. But they were in a world of their own just for these few minutes, and she was wildly, excitingly curious about him. Her fingers fumbled with the buttons until she had them open halfway down his chest. He didn't bother with undershirts apparently, and she smiled when she saw the broad expanse of hair-roughened skin.

His chest was rising and falling with his ragged breathing. She slid her fingers under the edges of the shirt and felt him go rigid. She touched the hard muscles slowly, caressingly.

He muttered something faintly violent, and all at once his hands went to the back zipper of her dress and slid it down to her waist.

"Cameron . . . !" she cried in a wild little whisper.

"I have to," he ground out, bending to her mouth. "Help me," he whispered against it. "I think I might die if I can't feel you against me this way!"

His mouth was making a slave of hers, and she was helpless to stop his practiced hands from pulling the dress to her waist. He brought her inside his shirt, groaning when he felt her bare skin uniting with his own, soft pink flesh melting into bronzed muscle.

Her throat ached with the tiny cry she made, and her hands lifted to his thick dark hair, tangling in it, holding her mouth to his as his body rippled against hers. She felt his hands move to her sides, caressing her in slow, bold sweeps that eventually led him to her high, taut breasts. She moved back a little, just enough to let his hands find her, and she moaned harshly at the unfamiliar, unexpected pleasure of letting him explore her so intimately.

He lifted his head to look at her while his thumbs rubbed with maddening leisure against the hard nubs. "You're exquisite, Merlyn," he whispered. "Magic and madness and silk to touch. And if there was a lock on this door, I'd have you right here on the floor, you know that, don't you?"

"Yes," she whispered, aching for that, aching for him. She wanted him with a shocking madness, blind to sense and reason. She was feeling sensations she'd never even dreamed of, and he was pleasing her in incredible ways. "Kiss me again," she begged.

"I wouldn't dare," he whispered back, his eyes fixed on the sight of her pale flesh against the dark skin of his hands where he was touching her. "My God, you're everything a man could want."

The sudden sound of a voice froze them both. Cameron scowled, glancing toward the closed door in slow motion. All at once, he seemed to realize that the sound was coming nearer. He let her go and stood there like some exquisitely masculine conqueror—his shirt undone, his hair mussed and his eyes blazing with frustrated passion. He was the handsomest man she'd ever seen.

"Pull that up," he growled, staring pointedly at her bodice.

Belatedly, she jerked it up and fumbled behind her for the zipper. Someone was at the door now—drunk from the sound of his voice—and the doorknob started to turn.

Cameron grabbed it and held it. "What do you want?" he asked curtly.

There was a pregnant pause. "What . . . do I want?" the voice mumbled.

Cameron's eyes twinkled. "That's right. What do you want?"

"My raincoat!" came the belligerent reply. "It's raining cats and dogs again, just like when I got here!"

"What color is it?" Cameron continued.

"Uh . . . brown."

He turned, glancing down the row of coats. "There are a lot of brown raincoats in here. What does it look like?"

"If you'll let me open the door," the slurred voice said, "I'll show you."

"Can't do that," Cameron said, glancing down at his own untidiness. "You describe it."

Merlyn had her face in her hands, trying desperately not to giggle.

The voice sounded affronted. "Of all the silly . . . all right, it's got epaulets and one of them is half off, and it's . . . it's a trench coat."

Cameron riffled through the coats and found the right one. He grinned as he took it off the hook, opened the door slightly, and flung it out, closing the door quickly again.

"Thash it!" the drunk chuckled. "Say, are you one of those automated closets?"

"You got it," Cameron agreed, holding the door shut. "Just installed. Brand new."

"Well, you work real good. I saw a talking Coke machine once. Say, you got any Cokes in there?"

"Fresh out. Sorry."

"Do you sing jingles?"

Cameron looked hunted. "Buzz off."

"Machines aren't supposed to be rude," the voice replied. "I'm going to report you."

"To whom?" Cameron asked politely.

There was a long silence.

Cameron glanced at Merlyn. "Why don't you report me to Mrs. Thorpe?" he suggested.

"Good idea!" There was the sound of footsteps receding. Cameron rushed to button up his shirt and vest and dinner jacket.

"Your hair," Merlyn said.

"Yours is just as bad," he murmured, looking down at her. "Well, there's nothing to be done about it now."

"No, I don't suppose so." She felt terribly shy with him now, self-conscious. She couldn't even lift her eyes as he opened the closet door. She brushed past him and made a wild dash up the stairs toward the bedrooms before anyone could see her.

As she made it out of sight, she could hear a voice muttering, "It did so talk! Come with me, I'll show you!"

She barely made it into the privacy of her bedroom before she burst out laughing.

It was several minutes before she felt calm enough to go back to the party. Her knees were still a little shaky, but her logical mind had forced her to see the disastrous path she was walking. Getting involved with Cameron Thorpe would bring nothing but heartache. He wanted her. But probably he was a passionate man who was capable of wanting any woman. Besides, there was Delle, whom he planned to marry. She had to remember that he might dally with a pretty girl, but he wasn't about to ruin his chances of marrying an heiress. Especially not with a woman he thought was a penniless historian. That was almost funny. But she wasn't laughing. What she'd felt in that closet had never happened before. And as she considered him with Delle, she colored and felt sick and empty. She hated the very thought of them together. But when she left her bedroom, at least she had her contrary heart under some measure of control.

6

The first person Merlyn ran into when she walked back into the spacious living room was Mrs. Radner. The older woman's eyes glittered unpleasantly, revealing her assumed smile to be as false as her geniality.

"There you are, Miss Forrest," she said, her chin lifting superciliously as she joined the younger woman. "I wondered where you'd gone. Cameron seemed to vanish at the same time, oddly enough."

Well, there was no better way to play it than with innocence, Merlyn decided. She smiled coolly. "Did he?" she asked. "How strange. I didn't see him."

Merlyn's poised self-assurance seemed to stun the other woman. "But you left the room together," she insisted.

"Did we? I didn't notice." Merlyn sighed. "I was so

desperate to get to my room. . . ." She smiled demurely.

"Oh." Mrs. Radner followed her lead, obviously getting the fake message loud and clear.

"Mr. Thorpe would hardly follow me, you know," Merlyn volunteered. "After all, I'm only the hired help."

Mrs. Radner nodded graciously. "Of course, my dear. There's Cameron now, dancing with Delle." She sighed, complacent now. "Don't they go well together? I've always adored contrasts."

They were a contrast all right. Cameron was dark, and Delle was fair. They made a handsome couple at first glance. But their steps didn't seem to match, and his arm was far too loose around his fiancée's waist. Added to that, Merlyn thought with helpless satisfaction, he still looked frustrated.

"Hello, dear, I lost you," Lila said, joining them. "We very nearly had a problem a moment ago."

"We did?" Merlyn asked.

"Yes." Lila frowned. "Some rather intoxicated gentleman kept insisting that the closet was automated and spoke to him." She stared at Merlyn. "Do you suppose he was having a religious experience?"

It was a credit to Merlyn's early training that she didn't drop to the floor and roll over with laughter. She managed to keep a straight face. "I hardly think so," she replied. "I've heard that heavy drinkers sometimes have hallucinations. Isn't that so, Mrs. Radner?" she asked with polite deference.

"I'm sure I wouldn't know," Mrs. Radner replied indignantly.

"Anyway," Lila concluded, "he's gone home, thank goodness. It was rather embarrassing, the way he kept dragging people into the hall to hear my closet talk."

Merlyn murmured something appropriate and escaped to the punch bowl. The band was just starting into a slow, easy tune when she noticed her friend Dick Langley leaving the group and making his way toward her. His blue eyes twinkled as he grinned down at her.

"How about a dance? One of the guests plays drums as a hobby and asked to sit in. It was truly my pleasure." He held out his arms.

She put down the glass of punch she'd poured and let Dick sweep her out on the dance floor. "We haven't danced together since the charity ball last spring," she murmured.

"No. I've been busy lately. What in the world are you doing here?" He glanced around. "My God, your father could buy and sell anyone here. Why are you hanging out with this bunch?"

"I'm researching for Lila Thorpe," she said with a grin. "And having a ball irritating her son. That's him over there with the ravishing blonde."

"She may be ravishing, but her vocabulary is limited to *yes, no,* and *oh, my!* And she seems to have a great fear of mussing her hair or makeup." He chuckled at Merlyn's puzzled look. "I asked her to dance a few minutes ago. Just after you vanished with the big man."

"He was showing me his etchings," she said.

"I bet he was showing you a lot more than that,"

he murmured dryly, "if the expression on his face when he came back was any indication. His girlfriend positively glared at him."

"I didn't think she knew how," Merlyn said contemptuously.

"Meow."

She sighed. "I can't help it. She's either hopelessly naive or shrewdly vicious. I haven't decided which. She made a nasty remark about Grandmother's pearls."

"The Forrest pearls," he murmured, glancing down at them. "They suit you."

"They suited her, too." She smiled. "I was just a little girl when she died, but I still remember how she used to make her grand entrance, always in some snowy white gown, wearing these pearls and carrying a colorful boa. She could have stopped traffic with her black hair and her blue eyes. . . . I miss her, Dick."

"Yes, I know. So does your father."

"Seen him lately?" she asked.

"Last week, in fact. He's missing you. Something about a party that needs organizing, and he doesn't trust Kitty to handle it."

Kitty was her father's secretary, a whiz with a computer but a total failure at organizing parties.

She smiled. "I'll volunteer if I win the bet I've got going with him."

"Bet?"

She ignored him. The thought of leaving was suddenly unpleasant, bet or no bet. And she only had a little over a week left. She'd grown very fond of Amanda and Lila. And him . . .

She shrugged. "A private joke," she murmured with a smile. "Anyway, I don't have much longer. Another week should do it," she said.

"Suppose we get together some weekend? I'll bring Bruce and Annie along and we'll go sailing down to Nassau."

"That sounds lovely." She liked their friends Bruce and Annie, and Dick was good company. He never insisted on getting intimate. That was the nicest thing about him, that he could be just a friend.

"Uh-oh," he sighed. "Time's up. My friend's losing his grip on the drumsticks." He stopped dancing as the song ended, bowed and kissed her hand. "*A bientôt, ma belle.*"

"*A bientôt, mon ami,*" she returned with a smile.

He left her and as she turned back to Lila, she couldn't help noticing Cameron's killing glare. It filled her with mingled satisfaction and apprehension. Her eyes narrowed as they met his. He needn't think he owned her because of one kiss, she thought angrily. Even if it was a kiss that led to much wilder explorations. She wasn't going to supply what his sweet Delle couldn't; she wasn't going to spend her life hidden away in closets. Closets. She sighed and shook her head. That was desperation. And remembering the shared urgency that had driven them to it, she shuddered. She'd never felt such abandon in her life.

Somehow she wound up standing with Lila and Cameron and Delle, although she'd done her best to avoid it. She couldn't help wondering if the Radners would go back to Atlanta that night.

"It's simply been a lovely party, Cam," Delle

sighed. "I'm really sorry about our car breaking down, but you don't mind having us for the night, do you?"

"Don't be silly, of course not," he said.

"Tell me about your friend Dick, Miss Forrest," Delle asked suddenly. "You seemed to know each other very well."

"Why, yes, we do," Merlyn told her. "He took me to my senior prom. A wonderful man. Very masculine."

"Is he a professional musician?" Delle asked with a mocking smile. "I've never met a real one before. Mother doesn't like me to associate with those kinds of people."

Merlyn almost went into gales of laughter, thinking about Dick's wealth. But she restrained herself. "He's very good, don't you think? And so good-looking," she sighed, noticing Cameron's dark glare out of the corner of her eye.

Mrs. Radner joined the small group, looking restless and perturbed. "Cameron, dear, was it necessary to invite so many people? I'm still searching for a familiar face."

What she really meant was that there were very few of "her class" around. Merlyn grinned. She'd noticed that Lila had invited several friends who weren't on the social register, and she admired her for her democratic spirit.

"You might enjoy meeting some new ones," Lila said pointedly. "Money doesn't necessarily ensure intelligence or talent, my dear."

"No, but it does usually ensure a measure of

breeding," Mrs. Radner said coolly. She glanced at Merlyn's gown with a practiced eye. "I was just noticing your gown, Miss Forrest," she said with a faint smile. "Last year's, isn't it?"

"No." Merlyn smiled. "It's this year's. Dick brought it for me."

Mrs. Radner's face closed up, as if any woman who allowed a man to bring her such a dress could only be one thing.

"Cameron, you really must get to know Dick," Delle murmured wickedly. "Perhaps he could show you where to get one for me."

Merlyn could have mentioned that it came from her home, but she wasn't going to give the show away this early. She glanced at Cameron's black scowl and decided that it might be wise for her to leave the premises for the rest of the evening. Sooner or later, the guests would leave, and Delle, her mother and Lila would go to bed. She was afraid of finding herself at Cameron's mercy a second time in one night. He was potent and she was all too vulnerable. And she didn't want to become a notation on his page of easy conquests. She knew what he was thinking; she could see it in his eyes. *Later,* he was telling her, *you and I have something to finish.* But she wasn't playing his game. Unfortunately, she'd given him the impression earlier that she was willing and easy, and it might prove difficult to convince him in time that she was neither. Getting away was the most logical move under the circumstances.

She excused herself, ignoring Delle's provocative remark, and moved to the bandstand, where the band was just ending a number.

"Can I leave with you?" she asked Dick in a whisper.

"Sure. In trouble?" he asked.

She sighed and smiled. "Up to my dainty ears. And make it seem blatantly clear why we're going, could you?"

His eyes twinkled. "Got you."

She kept well away from Cameron and the others until the party was over and the band started packing away instruments. Then she left with the band, clinging to Dick's arm as they passed Lila.

"Good night," Merlyn told her employer, as an angry Cameron came forward with a puzzled Delle in tow.

"Good night, my dear." Lila grinned. "Have fun."

"Let's go, Dick," Merlyn said quickly.

"I'll bring her back before morning," Dick said and pulled her close. "Good night, Mrs. Thorpe, Mr. Thorpe, ladies." At his most charming, he bowed and closed the door behind them.

"Whew!" Merlyn sighed as she sat in the van with Dick, the other band members and all their equipment. "Talk about close calls!"

"What happened?" Dick asked.

"I had words with the master of the house," she lied. Well, it was almost the truth.

"Odd," he murmured, raising his eyebrows, "I didn't think you saw him again after we danced."

"I was just avoiding trouble," she sighed, leaning heavily on his shoulder. The van was carpeted, thank goodness, so her dress wouldn't suffer.

"Sorry about the transport. I left my Jag at Ray's house. We'll pick it up when we drop him off."

She smiled. "It's just as well. They'd have been suspicious if they'd seen it."

"Don't I look rich?" he asked pointedly.

"No. You look delightfully charming and debonair. But not rich." She glanced up at him. "Do I? Look rich, I mean."

"No. You look threatened." He pulled her closer. "Did he make a pass, little buddy?"

"You see too much," she grumbled.

"I've known you since grade school, of course I do. Come on, spill it."

"Yes, he did. I'm still pretty raw after Adam," she confessed. "And this very staid banker has his eye on an investment firm."

"The blonde?"

"Her father owns the firm. He'd like to merge with it. By marrying her." She moved her dark head restlessly. "Not for love, you understand. He doesn't trust emotion since his disastrous first marriage, so he's marrying for logical reasons this time. His poor little daughter! She doesn't like the blonde at all."

"Poor you," he corrected. "You're falling for the guy, aren't you?"

She laughed dully. "I think it's psychological. The house is so much like Thornfield Hall in *Jane Eyre*, and I met him suddenly in the middle of the night . . . maybe it's just my wild romantic streak acting up." She pressed close to him. "Don't bother about me, I always get my act together eventually. Where are we going?"

"After we get off the bus? Oh, I thought I'd take you to Limelight."

It was an Atlanta club with good food, good music

and bright lights. "I'd love it," she said enthusiastically. "I feel as if I've been hibernating. Will I do like this?"

"You'll simply raise eyebrows, and I'll grin at your radiance," he returned. "You'll do fine."

She did raise eyebrows, but she had a wonderful time. She even managed to get Cameron out of her brain for whole minutes at a time. Admittedly, her fear of facing him was the main reason she stayed out so late with Dick. It was almost four o'clock when she got back to the house.

"I didn't realize it was so late," he said ruefully.

"Well, an hour to get there and an hour back," she reminded him. "Plus the time in the middle. It doesn't matter. I enjoyed it."

"So did I." He bent and kissed her cheek. "*Ciao*, love."

"See you. I'll make sure you're on the guest list for Dad's party," she added with a grin.

"You'd better!"

He drove off with a wave of his hand, and Merlyn walked quietly in the front door. She was surprised that it wasn't locked, until she entered the brightly lit hall and heard noises coming from the den.

"Cameron, don't," Delle was saying. "Honestly, you know I don't like being kissed so roughly. And you've mussed my dress!"

"It will press," he muttered.

"Stop that!" Delle burst out. "Cameron, what in the world has gotten into you tonight?" There was a flurry of movement, and Delle stormed out into the hall, disheveled and flustered. She stopped dead when she saw Merlyn, and Cameron came out behind her, his eyes flaring as he spotted Merlyn standing frozen in the hallway.

His very appearance spelled trouble. He was wearing his dress slacks, but he'd shed his jacket and vest, and his white shirt was open all the way down the front over that sexy broad chest. His hair was ruffled, his eyes glittering. He looked very much as he had in the closet, and she knew why.

The thought infuriated her, especially when he smiled in a mocking, superior way.

"Just getting in?" he murmured.

Merlyn felt her blood pressure shoot straight up. She wanted to hit both of them. She couldn't remember ever having felt such murderous rage in all her life. Her eyes blazed with green fire in her white face.

Cameron's expression suddenly altered, puzzling her, as she lifted her chin proudly.

"I see I wasn't the only one enjoying myself," she commented, staring pointedly at Delle's swollen mouth. "Of course, you two are engaged, aren't you?" she added with rare venom and a cold smile. "Anything goes these days."

She started past Cameron, and her expression made him flinch almost imperceptibly. "Good night, Mr. Thorpe," she said politely. "Miss Radner."

Delle was giggling, although it sounded as though it was prompted more by nervousness than humor. Cold fish, Merlyn thought. She ascended the stairs as gracefully as her mother ever had, though she had to fight to keep her spine from stiffening with anger. She didn't look back once, although she imagined she felt eyes watching her. Delle's girlish voice floated up in excited whispers, but Merlyn couldn't make out the words. She went straight to her room, locked the door and bolted it.

She didn't understand why she cried. It wasn't like her at all. But her mind kept going back to Cameron's surprising ardor. She'd once thought him a cold man, but her opinion had reversed quite dramatically. He was as potent as aged wine, and she could still remember the touch of his hands, even after taking a hot shower and two aspirin to help her sleep. She tossed and turned wildly, picturing him over and over again holding Delle, kissing her, touching her as he'd touched Merlyn.

"Libertine!" she muttered harshly and buried her tearful face in her pillow. It was dawn before she finally managed to sleep. And almost noon before she woke up.

She dressed in a pair of gray slacks and a candy-striped blouse to go downstairs, putting her dark hair in a bun on top of her head. She felt old today. Old and betrayed, although why she should feel that way about Cameron Thorpe, she didn't know. He and Delle were engaged, for God's sake! What business of hers was it what they did in private?

"Good morning, dear," Lila called to her from the study. "I didn't want to wake you. Cameron said you'd come in quite late."

She felt her face go rigid, but she managed a smile, just the same. "Yes, I did. Dick and I went dancing in Atlanta."

"Did you have a good time?"

"Very nice, thank you." She sat down. "Have you already started without me?" she asked, glancing toward the small computer screen.

"Just a few lines to get the feel of the next chapter. Here," she said, indicating a diagram. "This is where I'd like to jump to next."

"The wedding of Henry the Seventh and Elizabeth of York." Merlyn nodded. "That was an exciting period. Did you ever read about the interesting plots hatched against Henry by his mother-in-law, Elizabeth Woodville, and his wife's aunt, Margaret, Duchess of Burgundy? They make fascinating reading." She began to relate them, and Lila listened avidly, bursting into laughter when Merlyn finished. "Oh, yes, get that all down for me, please. I'll find some way to incorporate it into the story line."

"I thought you might like it." Merlyn frowned, suddenly aware that she hadn't seen Amanda. "Where's Amanda?"

"She went to Atlanta with Cameron to put the Radners on a plane to Charleston."

"My late grandmother was from Charleston," Merlyn said. Her eyes narrowed. "*She* had breeding and elegant manners."

"And the Radners don't," Lila murmured dryly. "No, you needn't apologize," she said, stopping the quick reply forming on Merlyn's lips. "I'm well aware of the failings of my future in-laws. They do rather cast a shadow on that city of cities."

"Well, with all due respect," Merlyn sighed, "I hope they won't be back before my work here is done."

Lila started. "You aren't anxious to leave?" she asked.

Merlyn looked down at her hands. "I have . . . other commitments," she murmured, remembering that she needed to phone her father today about that party. "I've enjoyed this very much, but you're very nearly at the point where you won't require my services further. And if you need anything additional, you can always phone me."

"I've grown fond of you, Merlyn. I'd hate to think that we were going to lose touch." Lila's wise old eyes searched the younger woman's. "Is it Cameron? I realize he's made it difficult for you here."

"He doesn't intimidate me," Merlyn said smoothly. "Not at all."

"He intimidates Delle, though," Lila murmured. "He was about as friendly as a heated lobster this morning. Much more irritable than usual. You didn't have words with him?"

"Not at all. He and Delle were still up when I came home." Merlyn yawned and stretched with pretended indifference. "I just said good night and went to bed."

"He was quite curious about your friend Mr. Langley."

"Was he?" Merlyn asked. She glanced at Lila. "Not his kind of people, of course." She gasped as she realized the implications of that sarcastic remark. "Oh, I didn't mean that."

Lila smiled. "You don't know Cameron. He doesn't choose his friends for social position or wealth. He never has."

"He's marrying Delle for her father's firm, though, isn't he?" Merlyn asked curtly.

Lila's eyebrows rose. "Is he marrying her? Lately I've been having doubts."

"You wouldn't if you'd seen them this morning," Merlyn muttered.

Lila laughed softly. "Oh."

She put so much expression into that single syllable that Merlyn actually blushed. She got up. "I'll go and get my books and be right back," she said quickly.

Her face was still burning when she got to her room. She didn't care about that big ape. She didn't! But why had it hurt so much to see him that way with Delle? She closed her mind to it and went back downstairs with her arms full of books.

Cameron didn't come back until late afternoon. Amanda ran alongside him, her arms full of boxes, her eyes flashing with laughter.

"Hi, Grandmama!" she called. "Look what Daddy bought me! I've got worlds of dresses, and new slips, and even a pair of jeans! I must go up and try them on right now, to show you!"

Merlyn was sprawled on the carpet with a book about the house of Tudor. She glanced up as Cameron walked into the room but quickly turned her eyes back to the book.

"Have a good trip, dear?" Lila asked. "Amanda seems rather excited."

"We went shopping," he said. He stood in the doorway, hands in his pockets, and stared at Merlyn for so long that she got to her feet in self-defense. Her heart was beating wildly. Her eyes glanced off his as she dropped into a chair near Lila's desk.

"No date tonight, Miss Forrest?" he asked with cold sarcasm.

"No date, Mr. Thorpe," she replied sweetly. "Some of us work."

His dark eyes narrowed. "Would you care to elaborate on that?"

"We've just finished a chapter," Lila said, pulling out the diskettes before she turned off her computer and printer. She put the diskettes carefully into their jackets and then into their box. "Have to be so careful with these little devils," she murmured. "But it's worlds faster than a typewriter. Did the Radners get off all right, dear?"

"Yes. They sent their regards, Miss Forrest," he added, perching himself on the corner of the desk. "Since you weren't available when they left."

"How polite," she said quietly. She glanced at him, her eyes approving his beige slacks and patterned brown shirt. He looked all male in casual clothes, and she remembered suddenly the way his skin felt under his shirt. It was all she could do not to catch her breath at the memory.

"We'd better go into the dining room for dinner," Lila said, glancing at her watch. "I'll just fetch Amanda."

Merlyn stood up, but Cameron blocked her path.

"I wanted to say something to you in private," he said curtly. "About last night . . ."

"Now, don't you worry," she said with a honeyed smile. "I understand perfectly that you wouldn't want me to get my hopes up just because you kissed me. Delle has gobs of money and I'm penniless."

His chest rose and fell heavily, quickly. "What I wanted to say," he continued coldly, "was that Mother mentioned you were wearing a designer dress."

"I borrowed it," she said flatly.

"And you came back in a Jaguar," he added. "I'd like to know what's going on."

Her eyebrows arched. "Do you think I might be an eccentric millionairess?" she asked with a grin.

His dark eyes narrowed. "I'm beginning to wonder quite a lot about you, lady. You're too damned mysterious to suit me."

"Just the right woman for you, in fact, if you'd admit it," she sighed, batting her eyelashes at him. Bluff, girl, bluff, she told herself. "Well, the truth is, I have tons of money, and I'm in the market for a hunk who's good in bed and wants to take care of me. Interested?" she flirted.

His eyes roved slowly down her body and back up again. "I don't like the effect you have on me," he said quietly. "I've never gotten hot enough to drag a woman into a closet before."

Her face felt unusually warm. She dropped her eyes to his vest. "Really? How exciting! See, I'm getting to you, Mr. Rochester."

"Yes," he said, but he wasn't teasing.

"No need to worry, though," she said. "I'll be gone in a week, and you can get back to normal again."

"A week?" He scowled. "I thought you and Mother had barely begun."

"I work fast," she told him. "And shouldn't we go into the dining room?"

He reached out and touched her throat. Just that— warm, strong fingers moving gently on her skin. But it was enough to stop her in her tracks.

"I want you," he said in an odd tone.

She felt as if the breath had been knocked out of her. Her eyes stared up helplessly into his.

"You're totally unsuitable," he said. His breath was

coming hard now, quick. "Too reckless, too mercurial."

"Look here, buster, you're no bargain either," she said in a breathless tone. "You staid banker types leave me cold."

He shook his head. "I got you hotter than hell," he said in a gruff whisper. "I'd bet half my stock that you've never been that way with another man, either."

"I have!" she burst out, but she sounded and looked frantic, threatened.

"No," he breathed. "Where did you really go last night? Not to a hotel; you just wanted me to think that."

Her lower lip trembled. It wasn't fair! How could she think straight while he was touching her? "We . . . went to a nightclub."

His fingers moved lower, to the vee neck of her blouse, and traced its outline. "As I thought," he murmured. "A totally innocent evening."

She glared at him. "Yours wasn't," she ground out.

"But it was, Merlyn," he said quietly, and his chiseled mouth curved softly. "I kissed Delle twice and felt your mouth both times."

Excitement highlighted her high cheekbones, brightened her wide eyes.

"A virgin," he breathed angrily. His fingers moved up to catch her long hair in a grip that hurt, and his eyes stabbed into hers. "Damn you, Merlyn!"

"I didn't drag you into the closet!" she whispered on a sob.

"You came, though," he accused. "You came, and

you let me strip you and touch you . . . Oh, God, I could feel your skin in my sleep, you little tease!"

She was shaking now, trembling with mingled fury and fear and desire. "I'm not a tease," she bit off. "Let me go!"

His dark eyes narrowed menacingly. "What would you call it?" he demanded. He glanced down at her blouse. "You led me on, party girl."

"You were the one who started taking my dress off," she threw back, green eyes blazing. "Men are supposed to have some kind of control over themselves, aren't they?"

His eyes widened with disbelief. "You thought I could touch you that way and just break it off with no ill effects?"

Her voice faltered. "Couldn't you? Adam always . . . could."

He drew in a harsh breath. "Who's Adam?"

She lowered her eyes. "The man I was going to marry."

He stiffened. She glanced up at him, puzzled by the waiting stillness of his body.

"You were engaged?" he asked.

She nodded.

"And you're still a virgin?" he persisted.

She glowered up at him. "He didn't want me. Not that way, at least. He wanted . . . something my father had." That much was true; he'd wanted her father's millions. "But I thought it was just gentlemanly restraint that kept him so respectful of my body."

"My God," he said heavily.

"Are you shocked, Mr. Rochester?" she asked with a bitter little laugh.

His eyes met hers. "Yes. Shocked that any man could want something more than you."

Her lips turned up at the corners. "Thank you," she said with quiet pride. "It sounds trite, but I did need that."

He frowned. "Is that why you came to work for my mother? To recuperate?"

She nodded. "In a way. Could I go now?"

"Did you want him?"

That was a question she hadn't expected. Her lips parted, but no sound passed them. She searched his dark face and realized quite suddenly that she hadn't wanted Adam. She hadn't known what wanting really was until Cameron Thorpe dragged her into a closet and unzipped her evening gown.

"No," she said slowly. "I don't believe I really did."

"Did you love him?"

"I thought so," she replied with a faint smile. "I don't think I knew exactly what love was."

"Apparently you still don't know what sex is," he said flatly. "You'd better not let me go that far again, Merlyn, for your own protection. You're damned vulnerable with me."

Her eyes glittered up at him. "I didn't tempt you in the first place!"

"Like hell," he returned. "You were flirting for all you were worth."

"It's my way!" she flashed. "It's my defense mechanism! Most men run for the hills when I start . . ."

"I'm not most men," he said with menace in his deep, slow voice. "You throw me off balance and that's dangerous. I could get hungry enough not to remember Delle or your virginity."

"I'll keep my blouses fastened to the throat and dig out my chastity belt," she promised, easing away from him. "Don't you worry, sir, I'll do my best to protect you from yourself."

He cocked his head, eyeing her narrowly, as if he saw through the mask of her outrageous humor to the frightened woman underneath.

"After all, you have your life mapped out," she persisted, moving toward the door. "You might just remind yourself occasionally that you're engaged."

His bold, slow gaze moved down her body and back up again, and it was every bit as intimate as his touch had been the night before, in the hot closet. "Why did you let me?" he asked gently, capturing her eyes.

Her lips trembled. She couldn't get words past them.

"You were lucky," he said after a minute. "Damned lucky. Or hasn't it occurred to you that I wasn't going to stop?"

Her lower jaw dropped slightly. "You . . . we couldn't have!" she whispered.

He laughed humorlessly. "Like hell we couldn't." He moved closer, looking down at her from a disturbing proximity. "Didn't you know, my innocent, that people can do it standing up?"

She hated that mocking smile. She hated him, too, for making her vulnerable, for laughing at her. Her face flamed, and she felt her fingers itching.

He seemed to sense that, because he reached down and caught her fingers in his. "He scarred you, didn't he?" he asked suddenly. "You're as afraid of your own emotions as . . ." He didn't finish the sentence, but she could have done it for him: . . . *as I am of mine.* It was in his eyes, his face.

"I don't trust men anymore," she breathed.

"And I don't trust women." He looked down at her mouth and his breathing quickened. "Not one bit." His fingers tightened on hers.

"Cameron," she protested in a faint whisper.

That seemed to make it worse. With a rough sound, he lifted her by the waist until she was on a level with his hard, glittering eyes.

"I don't want you," he said coldly, desperately, as though he was trying to convince himself. "I don't want your madcap humor or your quicksilver tongue or this body that makes me ache when I look at it."

"Then let me go," she whispered. "And don't complicate things."

He drew her slowly against him, brushing her body over his. "Tell me you want to be put down," he challenged. "Tell me you don't want my mouth as violently as I want yours."

"You're a . . . levelheaded businessman. . . ." She faltered.

His head bent. His open mouth bit softly at hers, his breath came fast and ragged. "Open your mouth," he whispered gruffly.

"No . . ." It was more a moan than a protest. She tasted him, and felt the excitement all over again. His hands slid around her, bruising hands that lifted and stroked and made her burn with a thousand fires. With a wild little cry, her arms went up and around him and clung. They stood there, clinging, breathing, tasting each other in a fever of need while the grandfather clock in the hall struck and echoed in the silence.

When he finally lifted his dark head, her hands were tangled in his thick hair, her lips were red and swollen from the ardent pressure of his mouth.

"If I let go of you, will you fall?" he asked, sounding shaken himself.

She made a small negative motion of her head and tugged halfheartedly at his hands on her shoulders.

He let her move away. His eyes glittered, his face was hard and strained. He laughed suddenly, bitterly, and his eyes were frankly hostile. "My God, I'm shaking like a boy of sixteen with his first woman," he said on a harsh sigh.

She fought to keep the tremor out of her own hands. "I think . . . I should leave," she ventured.

He shook his head. "Not yet," he said softly. "Not yet. Don't run from me."

"You've got Delle!" she burst out.

"Why are you afraid?" he asked. His voice was casual, but his eyes weren't. "Is it because you think I'm looking for a last fling before I settle down?"

She forced her voice to remain steady. "I'm not wealthy," she said with a trembling smile. "I have nothing, except my income from jobs like this one. And you're after a brokerage firm, I believe? A financially beneficial marriage?"

"How did we get on the subject of marriage?" he asked after a minute. "I don't remember proposing to you."

Her eyes flashed with indignation. "God forbid," she said curtly. "I don't want to get married. Ever."

He studied her curiously. "Don't you want children eventually?"

The conversation was getting entirely out of hand.

"Lila and Amanda should be down any minute," she said.

"Talk to me!" he said shortly.

"About what?" She moved away from him with her arms folded tight over her chest. "Your life is mapped out, isn't it?"

He frowned as he watched her. "It was."

Her eyes sought his, and a wild kind of current linked them for an instant.

She whirled and rushed out the door into the hall just as Amanda and Lila came downstairs. She smiled like a grateful refugee and herded them into the dining room before Cameron could get out of the study.

It was an animated meal. Merlyn was livelier than usual, reminiscing about her college days and drawing out Lila about hers, while Amanda giggled. Cameron sat and watched and listened, unusually quiet. There was something in his eyes that frightened Merlyn. He watched her with an intensity that was frankly disturbing. It didn't help one bit when he announced that he was extending his visit that weekend, and wouldn't be leaving that night.

7

━•◦◦◦◦◦◦◦◦◦◦•━

That evening, while Merlyn and Lila worked in the living room, Cameron and his daughter played chess nearby. But, all the while, his black eyes wandered restlessly to Merlyn. She met that searching gaze once, and it took her breath away. He smiled, secretively, and went back to his game.

The next morning he showed up in casual slacks and a black and tan shirt and proceeded, with Amanda's help, to talk Merlyn into going for a walk with them. Lila was delighted to take a break, and told her so, adding her coaxing voice to theirs.

Merlyn was herded out the door with Amanda in tow.

"You like to walk, don't you?" Cameron asked, as they started down a wooded path that led around the lakeshore.

"Well, yes, but there's still a lot of research to do before the end of the week," she protested.

"Mother can use the break," he said.

Amanda was ecstatic. Apparently this was something her father didn't do often. The little girl walked beside him with a shy smile, and he smiled down at her.

"Having fun?" he murmured.

She grinned. "Oh, yes, Daddy," she said. "It's been ages since we did anything together."

He ruffled her hair. "It's been ages since I took any time off."

"We used to go fishing when I was little," Amanda said. "Merlyn, did your mother and father take you fishing when you were a kid?"

Merlyn sighed. "No, dear. My parents weren't the type. Dad was very much wrapped up in his work, and Mother . . ." She smiled at the memory. "Mother was a butterfly. She wouldn't have known which end of the pole to put in the water."

Cameron studied her curiously. "What did she do?"

"She was a housewife," she said, avoiding that hard look. "What did your father do?" she countered.

He grinned. "He raised hell, mostly."

"Was he a banker, too?" she asked.

"Yes."

"Granddaddy used to take me fishing," Amanda volunteered. "He got the hook caught in his trousers once, and another time he got his line tangled in a tree."

"And Amanda learned some new words," Cameron murmured dryly.

"Do you look like him?" she said.

He shook his head. "My father was slight. Brown hair, brown eyes. I take after my grandfather. He was French-Canadian."

The youngster's eyes darted up. "Merlyn, what did your ancestors do?"

She smiled slowly. "One of them was a soldier," she murmured, remembering Richard and the Crusades. "He did a lot of traveling."

"You speak of your mother in the past tense," Cameron observed. "Is she dead now?"

"Yes."

"And your father?"

"He lives in Atlanta. We're great friends."

"But you weren't always?" he said with a sharp glance, and she knew he was remembering what she'd said before about her father's negligence.

"No," she agreed. "We weren't always. We grew closer after my mother died. He grieved for a long time."

"Was she like you?" he asked suddenly.

She smiled. "She was beautiful," she said. "Blue-eyed, with black hair and skin like peaches and cream. I used to lose boyfriends to her, despite the fact that she was twenty-five years my senior. She was always laughing."

"I think you're beautiful, Merlyn," Amanda said. "Don't you, Daddy?"

"Shame on you," Merlyn chided her, "for putting your daddy on the spot."

"As it happens," he said, catching her eye, "I agree."

The look made her tingle all the way to her toes.

"How were you named Merlyn?" he asked.

"My mother had a passion for English legends. She was English, you see. Merlin, the magician of King Arthur's court, was one of her favorite characters. She thought the name delightful for a girl, with the change of a letter."

"Who was King Arthur?" Amanda asked.

Merlyn couldn't resist recounting the old legend, while the little girl listened, fascinated.

"Haven't you ever seen any of the plays or movies about King Arthur?" Merlyn asked.

"Oh, I've never been to a play," Amanda confided. "And Grandmama and I don't get to the movies very often. And Daddy doesn't like for me to watch TV."

Merlyn's eyes flashed as they met Cameron's. "How terrible."

"Maybe I've been too strict," Cameron mused. "It's just that I'm so busy. Too busy. That can change."

Merlyn looked back out at the lake, where birds were circling the water. A few speedboats were chancing the choppy waves that had been churned up by the wind. "It's none of my affair," she said softly.

"You should see the lake when it's covered with sailboats, Merlyn," Amanda sighed. "They're so pretty, like white swans."

"Do you sail?" she asked Cameron.

"I've never had the time to learn," he said. He stuck a hand in his pocket. The wind blew his dark, thick hair as they strolled down the wooded trail, and she watched him without wanting to.

"Making money must be very important to you," she ventured.

"In recent years it's been more a matter of keeping it than making it," he said.

"Daddy, can I spend the night with Dale?" Amanda interrupted as they came to a graveled driveway that went down to a brown cottage at the shore of the lake. "You said you'd think about it. Can I?"

He frowned. "What did your grandmother say?"

"She said I could if it was okay with you. Please? Dale's a nice girl, and her mother's a nurse, and they have to go home day after tomorrow."

"All right," he said, defeated.

"Hooray!" Amanda laughed. "Can I go and tell her? It will only take a minute."

"We'll wait for you by the fallen tree," he told her. "Don't be long."

"Yes, Daddy. Thanks!" And she was off like a gangly little pony, all legs and flying hair.

"Where does Dale live?" Merlyn asked, curious.

"In that house." He gestured toward the graveled driveway. "Come on, we'll cut through here."

"Don't you want to speak with her mother?"

He looked like a thundercloud. "I do not."

She followed along behind him through the woods, almost tripping over undergrowth, dodging branches, until they came to a clearing.

"Why not?" she asked breathlessly, when he stopped at a fallen pine tree.

"Because she's divorced, thinks she's God's gift to man, and the last time I came to get Amanda, she answered the door in a see-through negligee. Does that answer your question?" he growled.

She laughed softly. "Did it embarrass you?" she teased.

"Yes, it did," he said, surprising her. "I don't like being hunted."

There was no smile to soften the statement. She studied his hard face and felt sorry for him.

"Is a woman's body so alarming to you, Cameron?" she asked.

He studied her for a long moment before he spoke. "My wife," he said quietly, "used what I felt for her like a weapon. She knew I wanted her. She liked to show me what I was missing, and then go cold and laugh at me. Some things that other women do remind me of that. I'm not a stuffed shirt, Merlyn. But I'm proud. Too proud, perhaps."

She felt sick at the thought of any woman treating him like that. It explained so much.

"How long were you married?" she asked, her voice soft.

"Six years," he replied. "But we stopped being lovers after the first year. When she got pregnant with Amanda, she raged at me for days. After the baby was born, I was given the choice of either having some minor surgery to prevent any future accidents, or giving up the marriage bed." He bent his head momentarily, then met her eyes. "I told her what she could do with her body. And I left her to her lovers."

She stared down at the ground. "I knew that there were women like that," she said after a minute. "I had a girlfriend once who used to brag about how she kept her boyfriend in check by using sex as a weapon. I thought it was cheap and vulgar."

Her opinion seemed to surprise him. He sat down on the tree and stared at her. "Wouldn't you do the same thing to get your way?" he asked.

She shook her head. "Afraid not." She glanced at him with a wry smile. "If what I felt with you in that closet is anything like the real McCoy, Mr. Thorpe, I don't think I'd be capable of holding out."

He burst out laughing, in spite of himself. "Hell!"

"Well, you asked," she reminded him. "I may be a virgin, but I'm not a prude."

"Are you curious about it?" he asked.

"Yes, of course," she replied honestly. "But to me it means commitment, you see. And I've never wanted anyone enough to go the whole way." Her face clouded. "After Adam, especially."

"What did your father have that Adam wanted so much?" he asked.

"Some stock," she said.

His eyes narrowed. "He's not a poor man, then."

"He's comfortable," she said, crossing her fingers behind her. He was that, all right. Very comfortable! "Any more questions, Mr. Thorpe?"

"I'm curious about you, Merlyn," he said quietly. "I don't like puzzles."

"So conventional," she sighed. "You just don't like me, because I'm a free spirit. I'd go swimming in the nude or play my guitar in public if I felt like it. I've even gone on the stage once or twice in community playhouses. But you wouldn't do any of those things, would you?"

He shook his head. "Afraid not. I'm inhibited."

"Except in closets," she murmured dryly, and then flushed. She jumped to her feet.

He was next to her immediately, pulling her against him. She wouldn't look up, but she could feel his breath on her forehead, smell the spicy cologne he wore, sense the warmth of his powerful body.

"Only with you," he whispered. His breath came jerkily. "I've never wanted any woman this much."

She put her hands against his shirt front, liking the feel of the hard muscles. "I won't sleep with you," she said matter-of-factly, although her heart was beating wildly. "That's right up front, and I mean it. No teasing, no games. If I ever give myself, it will be in love, and for life."

"What am I supposed to do?" he asked curtly. "Marry you to get you?"

"I don't want to marry you," she said. "You're too restrained for me, too wrapped up in making money. I want someone to play with."

"You're not a child," he scoffed.

"Yes, I am," she said simply. Her eyes traced the hard lines of his face. Impulsively, one slender hand reached up to touch his straight nose, his firm mouth. "I don't want to grow up if it means being staid and doing the correct thing all the time. I like my life as it is."

"I feel the same about mine. So does Delle," he added curtly.

She smiled sadly. "Then marry her."

His jaw tautened. His arms crushed her into his body, and he watched her face as his head began to bend.

"Don't," she pleaded gently. Her hands went to his hips to try to move them away.

The reaction she got was shocking and a little intimidating. They were so close that she could feel what was happening to him, and a tiny gasp left her lips.

He laughed despite his evident hunger, but he wouldn't let her go. "Calm down," he murmured. "Just because I'm capable, doesn't mean I'm going to throw you on the ground."

She swallowed, feeling threatened. "Let me go, please," she begged.

"Merlyn," he chided gently. He searched her eyes. "Are you really so embarrassed?"

"Yes!" she burst out.

He drew in a slow breath and let her move away, but only enough to satisfy her outraged modesty. "How old did you say you were?" he said in amazement.

Her darkened green eyes lowered in embarrassment. He tilted her face up, and his smile faded. He seemed to find something in her face that fascinated him, awed him. His dark eyes held hers for a long moment. Then, with a strange, deep sound, he began to slowly unfasten the black and tan patterned shirt over his massive chest.

She watched his fingers, deeply tanned, slender fingers with flat nails, as they slipped the buttons out of their buttonholes.

"What . . . are you doing?" she asked, trying to inject reason into the situation.

"I'm going to teach you something new," he said in a deep, rumbling tone. "Come here."

He caught her face between his hands and brought it gently against the thick, curling hair and warm muscle of his chest. Slowly, achingly slowly, he brushed her nose, her cheeks, against his body, until the sensuality of it got through to her and she moaned. Her nails dug into him as she sensed what he wanted her to do, and she opened her mouth on his warm, damp skin.

His hands contracted in her hair and his body stiffened. Under her mouth, his broad chest was rising and falling with a sharp, irregular rhythm.

She drew back and looked up, wanting to see his face and what he felt. But there was no reaction in it. His eyes were dark and steady on hers.

"Do . . . do you feel it?" she asked hesitantly. "The way I do," she added, "when you touch me . . . in the same way?"

"How do you feel?" he asked.

Her lips tugged into a nervous smile. "Like I'm on fire, I guess," she confessed.

"That comes close," he said. He pressed her cool fingers to his body and bent to kiss her. "No," he whispered. "Not like that." His tongue probed softly at the line of her lips. "Do that to me," he whispered. "And I'll show you how hot a kiss can get."

She did. And he did. And around them the forest blazed with promise. Her hands tugged wildly at his thick hair as he lifted her. She arched, clinging, wanting him so much that nothing in the world seemed to exist except the torment they were sharing.

"I want you," she whispered brokenly. "I want you!"

"I want you, too," he murmured hungrily. His breath came in ragged jerks. "So much!" he whispered.

Her mouth opened under the expert probing of his, and she gave in completely. If there hadn't been the prospect of Amanda returning any minute, she knew that he could have laid her down in the pine straw and taken her. And she'd have gloried in every second of his possession.

A sound penetrated the silence. A sharp sound, like branches being snapped not too far away.

Cameron let her slide down to her feet, his eyes dark and watchful. He was trembling.

"Are you all right?" she asked dazedly, touching his strong chest.

He blinked, looking down at her blankly while he tried to catch his breath. His eyes seemed clouded, his face strained.

"What?" he asked unsteadily.

"You're trembling," she whispered, concerned.

He laughed shortly. "Darling, so are you," he replied. His warm hands held her shoulders. "With desire, Merlyn. Didn't you know?"

She felt gauche and unworldly, and she must have looked it. Tenderly, he bent and brushed soft kisses over her closed eyelids.

His eyes went down her body and back up again, undressing her. She knew he was remembering the way she'd been in her bedroom that morning when he'd come upon her fresh from her bath. He smiled slowly.

"Don't undress me like that," she burst out.

He chuckled. "I don't have to. I remember every inch of you."

"Cameron!"

"Cameron Edward," he said, moving forward again. "And yours? Your full name?"

"Merlyn Forrest St . . ." She caught herself, but not in time.

"What?" He was scowling now. "I thought Forrest was your last name. It isn't, is it?"

She backed away. "It is. I was thinking of something else."

He didn't come closer. His face closed up, but his eyes revealed his curiosity. "You'll tell me, sooner or later."

"I won't be here later," she reminded him. "I'm leaving at the end of the week."

"Are you afraid of my potent charm?" he murmured with a wicked smile.

"It's pretty potent, all right," she agreed honestly. "I'm still shaking."

"So am I," he confessed. He lit a cigarette, fumbling with the lighter and laughing, as if his own clumsiness amused him.

"Need some help?" she asked dryly.

"Touch me," he challenged, "and I won't need a lighter to start fires."

"Flatterer," she murmured.

Amanda came crashing through the brush. "Gosh, I went the wrong way," she called out, laughing. "Did you worry?"

"No, honey," Cameron told his daughter, throwing an arm around her. "Merlyn and I were busy talking."

"About what?" Amanda asked.

Cameron studied Merlyn over the young girl's head, and his eyes were still burning. "Just things," he murmured. "What time do you have to be at Dale's?"

"Six."

"Merlyn and I will drop you off on our way to Atlanta."

Merlyn looked at him in surprise. "Atlanta?"

"I have to go to a cocktail party. Business. I thought you might like to come with me," he said. His eyes were promising things she didn't even want to guess at.

"I don't know . . ." she said hesitantly.

"You'll be as safe as you want to be," he said quietly. "Come with me."

She sighed. She wanted to. It was stupid, but she did want to. "All right," she said, and turned away before he could see the pleasure on her face.

8

The cocktail party was small and elegant. Fortunately for Merlyn, only one person there recognized her. The elderly gentleman who monopolized her at the buffet was a friend of her father, and she'd known him since childhood.

"Why don't you want anyone to know who you really are?" James Dunfey asked in confusion. "I don't understand, Merlyn."

"Because I'm doing some fascinating research on social mores," she lied. "You can't give me away, Dunnie."

He sighed into his martini glass. "Oh, very well," he said, noticing the way Cameron was watching them. "But your friend there is suspicious. Cameron Thorpe, isn't he? I've done business with his bank. Shrewd businessman, Thorpe. I expect he'll boost the bank's assets more than adequately when he's had a few more years to work on it. Bad luck about his father borrowing himself out of his fortune. Idiot. Should have made his holdings over to Thorpe years ago, instead of overreaching on a gamble and holding out for immortality."

"Is the bank very badly in debt?" she asked.

"Not the bank. Thorpe. I understand he's already paid off a quarter of a million in debts, though. He's got a good head, he'll make it."

She sighed. She had known there were reasons for him to marry Delle. Good reasons. She felt empty all the way to her toes.

Cameron asked her about Dunfey as soon as they found a moment alone.

"Friend of yours?" he probed.

She avoided his hawklike stare. "Why? Jealous?" she murmured, peeking up at him with a smile. He looked devastating in his gray suit with a red tie and white silk shirt. The colors contrasted nicely with his darkness. "He is quite dashing."

He smiled. "Yes, I did notice that. But does he have the stamina?"

Her lips curled. "I don't know." She glanced at him. "Do you?"

His eyes began to burn, and his chest rose and fell heavily. "Is that an invitation, Miss Forrest?"

"I wouldn't dream of it! After all, there's my reputation to think of!"

He toyed with his drink as he studied her. "I am thinking of your reputation. . . . It needs a few spots on it." A corner of his mouth curved upwards.

She laughed breathlessly and found that her hands were shaking as she lifted her wineglass to her lips. She gulped down a swallow of wine and almost choked on it.

He smiled faintly. "What's wrong, Merlyn?"

"As if you didn't know, you big furry wolf," she accused.

"You seemed to like the fur well enough this afternoon," he reminded her with a slow grin.

"Can I help it if you have a sexy chest?" she murmured, glancing up at him wickedly. "I never liked hairy men before."

His nostrils flared as he searched her eyes. "I'm like that all over," he murmured softly.

Her lips parted. "Are you?"

His eyes narrowed. He fingered his whiskey glass thoughtfully. "You seem to be torn between seducing me and keeping me half a state away."

"Self-defense," she said honestly. Her eyes searched his face quietly, and she saw her whole world in it. A flash of lightning suddenly burst outside the window, and it was no more jolting than what she was feeling as she stared up into Cameron's dark eyes. She tried to breathe steadily.

He caught a strand of her long, clean hair and ran it between his dark fingers. "I keep an apartment here in the city," he said after a minute, seemingly out of the blue. "Just for business. I've never taken a woman there." It seemed important to him that she understand that.

Her lips parted under his steady appraisal. She wanted him. She loved him. Would it be so very wrong? Her eyes wandered slowly over him, savoring the sheer size of him, the barely contained muscles of his body. This was the twentieth century, as her friends kept telling her. Perhaps it would show him that marrying Delle was not the answer. Perhaps it would convince him that it was better to marry for love. . . .

He laughed at his own folly. "My God, do you hear what I'm saying? I'm standing in the middle of a roomful of people trying to get a virgin into bed with me." He drained his glass.

"You don't want me, then?" she asked slowly, staring into her half-full wineglass.

He seemed to stop breathing. His chest was still. And then it wasn't. It lifted and fell abruptly.

She glanced up. His broad, dark face was rigid with some violent emotion, and there was an unnatural whiteness around his compressed mouth.

"Yes, I want you," he said. Then he actually smiled. "Just for the record, what would you do if you were in that apartment alone with me? Would you be afraid?"

"We aren't, so there's very little point in speculating, is there?" she hedged. "Now shouldn't we circulate? After all," she added venomously, "Delle would be aghast at what you've been saying to me."

He drew in a slow, harsh breath. "Delle is aghast at the thought of anything remotely sexual, and you know it, don't you?" he asked with a cold smile.

"Yes," she said honestly. "I have a very clear picture of her. You may mold her into a sensible and practical wife, but she'll never satisfy you in bed." Her chest rose and fell quickly, and the words boiled out of her. "You're a passionate man. You'll hate living with an ice cube."

"At least I won't be vulnerable with her," he cut back.

"Vulnerable?" Her green eyes darkened. "You won't even be alive." She turned and walked away from him. She hated him. She hated Delle. She hated the whole situation. And the more she hated it, the more she drank. She sensed his eyes on her as she moved from group to group. She knew he was angry at what she'd said. Well, it was only the truth. He'd marry his precious Delle and spend the rest of his life regretting it.

She finished her fourth glass of wine and set the glass gently on the table. Stupid man, she thought viciously. Stupid, stupid man! She loved him, she ached for him, and she was ten times richer than damned Delle! If he wanted money, why didn't he marry her? She was about to start on her fifth glass when Cameron appeared at her side and caught her arm.

"You've had enough," he said curtly. "Let's go."

"I'm only getting started," she muttered.

"Don't make a scene, darling," he cautioned with blazing eyes.

"And embarrass you?" She laughed and tossed back her long, black hair. "How exciting."

"You forget, I'm used to embarrassment," he said with a cold smile. "My late wife was matchless at causing public scandals."

That sobered her as nothing else could have. She remembered what he'd confided to her about

Amanda's mother, about the way she'd teased him. It was a measure of his trust that he'd told her even that much. She was sure he'd never mentioned it to anyone else. She felt ashamed. She could never tease him the way his wife had, regardless of the provocation. She cared too much to hurt him deliberately.

"I'm sorry, Cameron," she said. Her eyes searched his. "I'm . . . just a little tipsy, I think."

"No harm done. Come on." He caught her arm, propelling her toward the door.

In what was a blur of motion to Merlyn, they said good night to their host and hostess. Merlyn rushed out the door without pausing to remember the storm and found herself quickly drenched by the driving rain. The suddenness of the soaking made her cry out, but she was already wet from head to toe.

"Good God, I forgot the rain," Cameron growled. He hesitated under the arch of the door, but when he saw her dress being plastered to her body, he joined her. "Oh, what the hell!" Reaching down, he swung her up into his powerful arms and carried her down the sidewalk to the curb where the car was parked.

He looked down at her, his black hair flattened against his broad forehead, his dark eyes glittering. "Well, we have no choice about going to the apartment now, do we?" he asked with a hard laugh. "We can't very well drive fifty-odd miles like this."

"No," she agreed quietly. "We can't."

He slid her onto the plush seat and closed the door before he went around and got in behind the wheel.

He drove just two blocks and turned the car into a parking garage under a fabulously expensive-looking condominium. A moment later he herded her into the elevator.

"The only regret I have is ruining your dress," he said on the way up. "I'll buy you another one, just like it."

She gaped at him, her wet hair plastered against her face, her dress clinging to every slender line of her body. And she felt beautiful. Reckless.

He opened the door to his apartment and guided her into the blue-tiled bathroom, with its wall-length mirror and gold-fixtured whirlpool and vanity. He turned to her, his eyes quiet, wary, as they wandered over her drenched garment. "I very much doubt that the clothes dryer's best efforts are going to do that any good," he said, frowning. "Mother has some jeans and a sweat shirt around here somewhere. You're just a little smaller than she is. Want to try them?"

"Yes, please." She was trying to sound sophisticated and worldly, but her voice betrayed her nervousness.

Cameron's clothes were plastered to him, too, emphasizing the sheer size of him, the straining of muscle against fabric. Her eyes sketched him, and she could almost picture him without clothes at all, his hair-roughened body bare to her eyes.

He noticed that quiet scrutiny, and his chest rose and fell roughly. "You can towel dry first," he said finally. "I'll wait."

Her eyes didn't leave his as she reached behind her for the zipper and slowly, gracefully, slid the ruins of her dress down to her waist, over her hips, and to the floor. She hadn't worn anything under it except briefs, and her long, slender legs were bare of hosiery. She eased off the briefs and her shoes, her heart beating wildly as she saw the astonishment in his dark face.

"Did you know," she managed breathlessly, moving slowly toward him, "that virgins sometimes seduce men?"

Her trembling fingers went to his jacket. Before her nerve failed, she started methodically removing it. Then his tie. His drenched white silk shirt. But her hands faltered at the belt.

His chest lifted and fell roughly. Without a single word, with a kind of fatalism, he held her eyes as he removed the rest of his clothes.

She went to him without fear, without reservation, her heart beating wildly, her body hungry for him. "Cameron," she whispered achingly. She pressed herself against him with the last tiny bit of courage she possessed. If he pushed her away, she'd die of rejection. "Cameron!" she breathed as she felt hair and muscle and bare flesh in a tremulous joining, and it was all of heaven.

His warm hands held her shoulders and he went rigid, as if he couldn't quite decide what to do. Against her, his powerful muscles clenched and she felt the bristly hair on his chest and stomach and thighs moving against her soft, bare skin.

"You're not quite sober," he reminded her in a voice taut with control.

"That . . . will help, won't it?" she asked shakily. Slowly, she lifted her eyes to his and gathered all her nerve. Her hands went to his thick, wet hair, and coaxed his face down to hers.

Her mouth assaulted his, and it was like fireworks

going off. He began to tremble as her mouth opened. Her tongue teased him, her body lifted and fell with the suddenness of desire as she registered his masculinity, the rich scent of cologne, the smooth tautness of muscle.

His hands skimmed her waist, her thighs, and then moved up her back in a long sweep. His mouth began to answer hers slowly.

She drew back, sure of her ground, sure of her own power. Delle wasn't going to get him without a fight. In her dazed mind, this was the only sure way to fight back.

She caught his big fingers in hers and tugged, drawing him toward the bedroom. He sat down on the big, king-sized bed, and she pushed him back against the pillows in a reclining position.

With more enthusiasm and love than skill, she eased herself down beside him and began to kiss him. She loved the taste of him, the magic of being intimate with him, seeing him as she knew Delle never had. And the incredible thing was that he let her. He lay quietly, his eyes open and dark with desire and frank astonishment, while she learned him with her hands and eyes. She bent her head and drew her mouth slowly, lovingly, across his hair-roughened chest, down to the clenched muscles of his stomach. He jerked convulsively.

"Merlyn!" he ground out, arching.

"It's all right." She laughed with a last surge of humor as she slid up the length of his body and kissed his hard mouth softly. "I won't hurt you, Cam," she promised in a loving whisper.

"Oh, God, honey, but I'll hurt you!" he murmured

harshly, even as his hands found her waist and lifted her, guided her. "Merlyn . . . !"

"You won't have to. I will. Let me," she whispered. He was sitting now, with her body easing down over him. With reckless hunger, she put her mouth to his as her hips moved. She gasped, hesitated, moved again, and her breath sighed out raggedly into his mouth. "It's all right now," she whispered then, and moved his hands to her hips. "Help me, Cam."

"You'll hate me," he breathed, but the fever was burning him. It was in his eyes, in the involuntary movements of his body, in the pressure of his fingers as they dug in and demanded.

"No. I love you," she whispered back, fervently, urgently. She felt him shudder as she put her mouth back on his. With innocent, unknowing ardor, she kissed him in a way that shattered his strained control. "Cam . . . ?"

His face held her fascinated gaze, and then it began to contort. His eyes closed. The powerful corded muscles of his neck strained. His chest rose and fell with wild movements, and harsh, groaning sounds burst from his lips. "Merlyn," he whispered, trembling. His body moved, his big hands bruising her hips as they contracted suddenly. "Merlyn!" he cried out, arching, his muscles locked, his head thrown back against the pillows in an agony of completion.

She realized that she'd been holding her breath, and she let it out all at once, astonished at how easy it had been, at how wild his reaction was. She leaned down on his wildly shaking chest and took his damp face into her hands, gently kissing him. Her mouth brushed softly over his closed eyes, his cheeks, his nose, his chin, anywhere she could reach, while she gloried in the pleasure, the peace she'd given him.

"Darling," he whispered huskily. His eyes opened, dark with wonder. "Darling, darling!"

He crushed her against him, turning, stretched out fully so that she was beside him, under him, and his mouth found her flushed face, tasting every soft inch of it with a tenderness she'd never dreamed he possessed.

"I gave you nothing," he whispered, holding her eyes as he trembled against her in the aftermath. "Nothing!"

"Everything," she corrected breathlessly. "All I wanted was to please you."

He drew in a slow breath, searching her face slowly. "Why?"

She reached up and touched his mouth. "I love you," she said simply. "I wanted you to be the first, and the last. Oh, Cam, I love you!"

"Love me?" he asked, incredulous.

"Yes," she moaned. "I wanted to show you that relationships can't be mapped-out campaigns and logic," she said. She tangled her hands in the thick hair on his chest and tugged. "Are you sorry?" she asked suddenly.

"I'm too exhausted to be sorry," he said softly. "Lie down. I'm going to make it good for you."

"Now?" she asked, stunned, watching his face break into a faint smile.

"Yes," he replied gently. He bent and traced her mouth with his, inciting her, smiling against the soft movement of her lips as she reacted to the slow caress. "Yes, like that." His hands moved down, finding soft skin and hard peaks, and his eyes flashed violently as his hands contracted.

She arched, gasping, her hands clutching at his arms.

"Come to me," he breathed roughly, his eyes blazing with desire, with appreciation. "If you love me, show me."

She'd known for a long time that there was passion in him, but the passion he showed her then was as overwhelming as a flood. For minutes that seemed like hours, his mouth and his hands teased her, tormented her. She moved like a wild thing, all gasping cooperation, loving the feel and strength of him.

But when he nibbled at her breasts, she jerked. His mouth gentled her.

"Be still," he whispered. "This won't hurt, it's just love play. Do you like it, Merlyn?" he whispered as his mouth played over the peak of her breast and tested its tautness.

"Yes," she whispered on a sobbing breath. "Kiss me there," she moaned, lifting her arms to draw his head down.

His mouth did impossibly sweet things to her mind, her body, her nerves. She arched toward his lips, her hands holding on his face, her eyes wet with tears of agonized pleasure.

Eventually his head came up, and the air felt cool on her moistened flesh. She moaned in protest.

His hand was on her, stroking, his eyes there, too, seeing her helplessness, her vulnerability. She caught her breath, and drew his mouth against her flat stomach, loving the sensations she was discovering.

"You're as passionate as I am, aren't you?" he whispered roughly. His eyes moved back up to hers, and she felt him suddenly begin to tremble. "Fire and magic. And I'm going to satisfy you, darling. Now."

Her heart went out to him. She searched his dark, broad face, seeing his eyes in the dim light, his dark, beautiful hands on her body. And it occurred to her that there wouldn't be another man. Not ever. She loved him. If this was all she could have of him, this one night, she was going to make it a night that would last forever. For her whole life. And if there was a child, that would make it even more wonderful. She'd have a part of him that Delle wouldn't.

Her eyes were full of this new-found understanding; her body trembled with the knowledge of it. She reached up, very gently, as he moved down. He gave her the full weight of himself. And she gave him her mouth and her trembling body, all in one sweet, wild movement. And she soared and burned and whimpered, finally, as he gave her back the fulfillment she'd given him. And more.

They must have slept then, because when she opened her eyes again, there was a chiming sound somewhere nearby. It was still dark.

She blinked. The covers were over her, and a dark figure was standing by the window, staring out. She sat up, memory washing over her. Her face burned as she recognized Cameron's broad back. He was dressed in slacks and a sweater and was quietly smoking a cigarette.

The soft sound of her movement must have caught his attention. He turned, and what she saw on his face made her want to cry. Because it wasn't love and happy ever after. It was bitter regret. Anguish, almost. She knew without his saying anything that she'd failed miserably.

"Get dressed," he said quietly, moving toward the door. "It's going on midnight. We'd better get back."

She didn't look at him. She couldn't. She sat there with her head bowed as the door closed gently behind him.

Like a sleepwalker, she pulled on Lila's jeans and sweat shirt. They were loose on her, but it didn't matter. Her high heels would have to do for shoes. Lila's feet were much bigger than her own. She looked in the mirror and felt sick. She looked like a tart on the town. Her mascara had run, and her mouth was still slightly swollen from Cameron's passion. There was a mark on her throat that was unmistakable. She found her purse and combed her tangled hair over the bruise, hoping no one would notice.

Her hand trembled as it found the doorknob. She felt sick all over, burning up with regret and fear and self-contempt. She vaguely remembered whispering that she loved him. How was she going to face him? How was she going to go on living after tonight? Doubt and worry tore her apart. If she'd ever had a chance with him, she'd thrown it away tonight. How could she have been so . . . so . . . wanton?

She avoided his eyes as she clutched her purse and joined him in the living room.

"Ready?" he asked carelessly. If she had looked, she would have seen that his eyes were anything but careless.

"Yes."

She followed him out the door, shamefaced, her head bursting with pain.

It wasn't until they were in the car again that she felt his eyes watching her. She looked up, and he said something rough under his breath when he saw her face. His own was pale, his eyes bitter and cold.

9

He drew in slow, deliberate breaths, and his eyes held hers relentlessly.

She averted her face. "Do you hate me for what happened?" she asked quietly. She laughed bitterly even as his lips were forming a reply. "Well, don't worry, money man, you couldn't possibly hate me any more than I hate myself right now. It must have been the wine. I'm sorry I didn't realize what it was doing to me."

He pulled out a cigarette and lit it, his eyes dark with pain and regret as they studied the glowing tip. "So am I," he said after a minute. "You didn't use anything, I gather?"

Her eyes closed. "No."

He drew in a slow breath. "I suppose you realize . . ."

"If it happens, I'll cope," she said tautly.

"How?" he demanded, running an angry hand through his hair. "Oh, God, what a mess!"

Tears were rolling silently down her cheeks, tears he couldn't see because she'd turned away from him. She hadn't dreamed it would be like this, that she'd feel this emptiness afterwards, that passion could turn to bitterness so soon.

"Could we go back to the lake?" she asked after a minute, her voice husky but controlled.

"I'd rather we hashed this out first. It's something we can't talk about in company."

He made it sound like some sordid episode that would blacken his name forever. Perhaps he even felt that way, she thought. The tears grew hotter, more profuse.

"I'll have to leave immediately," she said after a minute. "I'll get my father to call and I'll tell your mother there's an emergency at home. It will be the best way. She's far enough along now that I can . . . Cameron!"

He'd jerked her face around, and his jaw tautened as he saw the tears staining her cheeks. "Oh, God, honey . . . !" he whispered achingly.

"I did it," she reminded him. She backed against the door, her lower lip trembling, her eyes brimming with more tears. "It was my fault. You don't have . . . a thing to feel . . . to feel guilty about. There had to be a first time, didn't there?"

He sighed heavily, angrily. "You told me once that the only way you could give yourself was in love, and forever. Remember?" he asked bitterly.

She swallowed a sob and turned her eyes away. The joke was on him. She had given herself in love.

But he wouldn't know that, because she couldn't tell him. Her eyes closed.

"I only want to forget," she whispered.

His face contorted. He reached for the ignition. "I hope it's as easy as you seem to think it will be," he said shortly.

"Yes, I imagine you do." She laughed, brushing away the tears.

His eyes darkened. He glanced at her. "What do you mean?"

"Your mother told me. About your financial woes." Exhausted, she huddled down in the seat. "Cameron, don't you know that if you marry for money, you'll never be able to live with yourself?"

"I'm not marrying for money!"

She searched his hard face, saw the flashing anger in his eyes. "No? What else has Delle got that you want?"

He turned away. "You'd better fasten your seat belt."

"Don't treat me like a child!"

"Then stop acting like one," he growled, glaring at her. "My life is my affair."

"Fair enough," she told him. She turned away and fastened her belt with a snap. "Consider my interference ended, permanently."

He put the car in gear with a glance in her direction. "I'd hoped we might iron things out tonight, solve a few mysteries," he said. "The one we solved wasn't what I had in mind, however."

"Is there any other?" she asked, trying to keep the thought of his lovemaking buried in her mind. He'd been so tender, so ardent . . .

"Your past," he replied. His eyes glanced toward her. "I had a talk with James Dunfey before I took that last glass of wine away from you."

She froze. "Did you?" She studied her hands in her lap. "What did he say?"

"That you were incognito and he wasn't telling me a damned thing. Then he grinned and told me all my financial woes were over if I had you in my pocket." His face hardened. "It made me mad as hell. That's why it was so easy to seduce me, little rich girl," he added with a hard glare at her shocked face. "I was knocked off balance already. Having you come at me without your clothes on was just enough to give you the edge. I didn't have a chance in hell."

Her teeth ground together. Damn Dunnie! "Did he tell you who I am?" she asked.

"No. He said you'd do that in your own good time," he replied. He sighed roughly. "Couldn't you even trust me that much? For God's sake, am I that hard to talk to?"

She tossed back her unruly hair with a rough hand. "I had a bet with my father that I could get an ordinary job and not revert to type," she said through her teeth. "Men only like me for my money, you see," she added venomously.

He lifted his cigarette to his mouth and glanced at her wryly. "Like hell. Your body is more than enough of a dowry. I could have died trying to get enough of you."

She flushed and chewed on her lower lip. At the moment, all she felt was shame and betrayal. Now she couldn't be sure if his interest was in her or her money. Despite the fact that he didn't know who she was, wouldn't it be enough that she was rich? She was good in bed, and Delle wouldn't be, so maybe he was willing to make a switch. But she didn't want him that way. She wanted him to love her for herself, and—thanks to Dunnie—now she'd never know if he did. Her eyes closed on a wave of pain. She was going to have to leave, and it would be the hardest thing she'd ever done. She loved him more desperately now than ever, having belonged to him completely. It would be like tearing her heart out.

"Nothing to say?" he asked.

She laughed bitterly. "What is there to say? If you want to marry money, I can buy and sell your icy girlfriend. So how do you feel about me now, Cameron?" she added with a cold smile in his direction.

His dark face hardened. "Disappointed," he said with an equally cold smile. "I thought you were a better judge of character. My mistake."

He didn't say another word all the way up I-85, not until he'd pulled into the garage and closed the automatic door behind them.

"Are you all right?" he asked finally, as if the words had been torn from him.

"Yes, thank you." She opened the door and got out, steady on her feet, and went toward the kitchen entrance. But as she started to reach for the doorknob, he was in front of her.

"Not like this," he ground out, his eyes haunted. "For God's sake, we can't just . . . !"

"Let me by, please," she said in an inhumanly calm tone.

"Will you listen to me for a minute?"

"There's nothing more to say. Just think of me as a one-night stand. Let me by, please."

"Damn you!"

He reached for her, but she jerked wildly away from him like a hurt animal at bay. Tears glittered in her eyes, along with pain and regret and fear. "I was drunk!" she burst out. "I made a fool of myself, all right? I'm very, very sorry that I seduced you! Now, please, may I go in the house? I'm cold!"

He stared at her with blazing frustration and anger. "Merlyn, we've got to talk!"

"I hate you," she whispered, and even meant it at the time. "You're nothing but a stuffed shirt with a cash register for a brain! You wouldn't recognize love if it built a nest in your hair. I hate myself for what I did tonight, and I hate you for letting me do it when you knew you only wanted me for my money, when Dunfey had already told you I was rich! Well, too bad, but now I know the truth, and you'll never get that close twice. I never want to see you again as long as I live, Cameron! Go marry Delle and her father's investment firm, and I hope you'll be very happy!"

He flinched as if she'd hit him, and she turned and ran into the house and up the stairs like a wild thing. She slammed and locked the door to her room, and cried until she thought her heart would break in half. It was ironic, she thought, that the first man she truly loved had to be a man just like Adam, one who wanted her for her wealth. She'd gotten over Adam, but she knew she'd never get over Cameron. Not as long as she lived.

10

Organizing her father's party kept Merlyn's mind busy. But the nights were still bad, despite the fact that it was almost a month since she'd left the lake house and Cameron behind. She wondered if he'd tried to trace her and smiled wistfully.

She missed Amanda and Lila, and wished that she could contact them, just to say hello. But that wouldn't be a good idea. Inevitably, Lila would mention Cameron, and Merlyn couldn't bear to hear his name. It would hurt too much.

She sighed as she looked over the guest list one last time. The invitations had already gone out, but she was checking to make sure she hadn't left anyone out. Had he searched for her? she wondered. Had he cared enough? Or had she really been just a one-night stand?

She still blushed when she remembered that wild

night, her own brazen behavior as she pulled off her dress and went to him, as she led him into the bedroom. It had been beyond her wildest expectations. And despite the fact that she had disregarded all her principles that night, a small part of her was glad that it had happened. She loved him. Not that loving made it right, but she'd known somehow that one night would be all she could have of him. One night, to last a lifetime. She laughed bitterly. She could never marry now, never allow another man to touch her as he had. It would probably amuse him to know she'd given him her heart along with her body. For her, it hadn't been just a night. It had been forever.

Sadly she shook her head, feeling the new length of her hair with nervous fingers. She'd had it cut to fall saucily around her face and neck, and she liked the look of it. She looked like something out of the Roaring Twenties. But the old gaiety had left her face, the dancing mischief had gone out of her wide eyes. She was a shadow of the carefree woman she'd once been.

"How's it coming?" her father asked from the doorway.

"It's done," she told him. "Right down to the band and the caterers. You, uh, did mean to invite the Radners?" she added, trying not to sound as if she minded.

His eyes narrowed. "Yes, I did. Afraid Thorpe will come with them?" he taunted.

She felt herself pale, but the eyes she lifted to his were brave. "Not in the least," she returned. "He wasn't invited."

"Yes, he was," he replied. He put his hands in his pockets and smiled slowly. "I phoned him."

The hands holding the list trembled. She lowered her face. "Did you?"

"And you're dying to know what he said, aren't you?" He chuckled. "He sounded pretty raw, if you want to know."

"Maybe Delle's giving him fits," she muttered coldly.

"Maybe you are," he said. "I'd bet odds that he tried to find you, even though he couldn't have known where to look. Apparently, you didn't tell anyone your last name. He was shocked to the back teeth when I told him who my daughter was."

"Whom shall I invite for you?" she asked, refusing to be baited.

"Maggie Blair," he said, naming an old friend and occasional dinner guest. "And who's coming for you?"

"Dick Langley," she said without hesitation.

"Is he still racing those damned cars?"

"He won the last race," she protested. "He's a nice man. Very rich. Great fun."

"And a dead loss," he scoffed. He cocked his head. "Why didn't you call him?"

"Dick?" she hedged.

"Thorpe!"

Her shoulders moved restlessly. "I don't like looking back."

"It's not my place to dictate to you," he said after a minute. "But if you get pregnant, he has the right to know."

Her face jerked up, and she paled. "But . . . !"

"Did you think it wouldn't show?" he murmured dryly. "You left here a little innocent and came back looking whipped and half alive. It didn't take much imagination to see how things went. Are you pregnant?"

"I don't think so," she said honestly, and with a faint smile. "But I wish I were. Does that shock you?"

"Not at all," he said, and smiled with genuine fondness. "I'd like a grandchild or two. But it would suit me better if you had a husband first."

"I could marry Dick."

"You could marry Thorpe. If he's as tormented as he sounded, he'd probably say yes if you asked him."

"He only says yes when he's seduced," she grumbled.

He laughed. "So that's what happened!"

"You always used to say, 'Go after what you want in the most straightforward way possible,' didn't you?" she asked innocently.

"It worked for me," he agreed, and winked. "How do you think I got your mother to say yes?"

"Dad!"

He turned away, laughing. "It will all work out," he said with characteristic smugness. "I know that, even if you don't."

He left, and she watched him with loving eyes. He knew her so well. It had taken years for them to build this relationship, but she was grateful for it. At least she had someone to run to, someone to talk to. She wondered how it would have been if she hadn't?

Her hand touched her stomach lightly. She hadn't thought much about pregnancy. She felt no different. It was too soon to tell, of course, but she hoped. How she hoped! If she couldn't have Cameron, his child would be almost as wonderful. She leaned back with a tiny smile and daydreamed about how it would be. Then she suddenly remembered that she hadn't phoned the florist. Well, there would be time to daydream later.

All too soon, the night of the party arrived, and Merlyn stood at the top of the staircase, looking down on the elegant guests. She was taking a page out of her mother's book, wearing a stark white gown that fell gracefully from a strapless bodice. For contrast she had added black high heels and a black fur boa around her bare shoulders. The saucy little hairdo suited the look, although, just this once, she missed the masses of hair that she had once piled into elegant coiffures.

Her eyes scanned the newcomers anxiously. Well, at least Cameron hadn't shown up yet. Perhaps he wouldn't come. . . .

She started slowly down the staircase, poised and graceful, and glad of her choice of gowns when her father looked up and grinned with pride.

She'd just reached the bottom step when the door opened to admit the Radners—Delle and her mother —and Cameron. Cameron was chatting with an acquaintance, and Merlyn's helpless eyes made a meal of him. He looked broader than ever in his tuxedo, darker and more masculine. His crisp black hair was slightly damp, as if he had been in the rain, and she remembered another rainy night. . . .

"Why, Miss Forrest," Charlotte Radner said with a

laugh, as if she were shocked to find Merlyn in such grand company, "how unexpected."

Merlyn's eyebrows rose with just the right amount of hauteur. "Mrs. Radner," she said, extending her hand. "We're delighted that you could join us."

Charlotte blinked, staring at the outstretched hand. She took it automatically.

"Dad," Merlyn said deliberately, "this is Charlotte Radner and her daughter, Delle."

"Charmed," he returned with a twinkle in his eyes. He lifted Charlotte's hand to his lips. "Merlyn has mentioned you both."

Charlotte looked as if she might choke, and Delle gaped.

"But your name is Forrest," Delle blurted out.

"My full name is Merlyn Forrest Steele," Merlyn said with quiet poise. "I use my mother's maiden name in my travels. You'd be amazed at how many people court me just because of my father."

Charlotte was pale. "Yes, I see," she managed. "How kind of you to invite us."

"Darling," Dick called, laughing, as he moved through the throng with a glass of champagne. He looked handsome in his pale blue tuxedo. "Here you are." He handed the champagne to her. "Mr. Steele." He nodded at her father. Then he grinned at the Radners. "How nice to see you again."

"You remember Dick?" Merlyn asked the women carelessly, smiling up at him. "He's the heir to the Langley fortune—oil, you know," she added. "When he isn't indulging his passion for formula racing cars, he sits in with a band in Gainesville."

"I always wanted to be a drummer," he confessed. He held out his hand. "Miss Radner, may I introduce you around?" he asked Delle. "Mrs. Radner?" he added with a pointed glance at Charlotte.

"How lovely," Delle said in an excited voice.

"You . . . will excuse us?" Charlotte asked, smiling wanly. She walked off with her daughter and Dick, looking as if she were choking on a watermelon.

"Feel better?" her father asked.

Merlyn shook her head. "Not much. I thought I'd enjoy it. I didn't."

"Better get yourself together. Here comes trouble," he said under his breath.

Cameron was just excusing himself to his acquaintance. He turned to greet Mr. Steele and Merlyn. And the look on his dark face was carefully controlled to show no emotion.

"Ah, Thorpe!" her father said with a beaming smile. He moved forward to take Cameron's hand. "So glad you could come! This is my daughter, Merlyn. I believe you've met?"

"Met is hardly the word," Cameron returned. His dark eyes narrowed, as though he could control himself no longer. "Do come and have a chat with me, little miss heiress."

"I have to receive my guests," she replied stiffly, frightened.

"How would you like to do it hanging over my shoulder?" he asked.

"I'd go, if I were you," her father advised with an amused glance. "You'd look pretty silly being carried out of here in a fireman's lift."

"Some help you are!" she accused.

Her father shrugged. "Don't blame me. You seduced him."

Cameron's eyes flared. "Well, I'll be damned," he burst out, glaring at her. "What did you do, come home and brag about your conquest?"

"You'd better keep your voice down, Mr. Thorpe, or Delle will hear you," she advised, struggling as he grasped her upper arm.

"Cameron?" came a plaintive little voice from behind him. Delle came up, glancing past him at Merlyn.

"What is it, Delle?" he asked as if he couldn't care less.

"Well, I just wondered if you wanted to come and have some punch," Delle said helplessly.

"Merlyn and I have things to talk about," he said shortly.

"What things?"

"Our baby, for one," he said as he stared into Merlyn's shocked face.

"Baby!" Delle burst out.

"What baby?" Merlyn asked.

"Oh, I happened to mention that you were pregnant," Mr. Steele said pleasantly, smiling at Merlyn with superb nonchalance.

"Dad!" she cried, aghast.

He shrugged, lifting his glass of champagne toward Delle. "Would you like to dance, Miss Radner?" he asked with a grin. "I'm pretty light on my feet for an old man."

And before Delle could say another word, he led her away.

Merlyn looked up at Cameron. "I don't care what he told you, I'm not pregnant."

"Aren't you?" he asked. His eyes wandered over her slowly. "How can you be sure? It hasn't even been a month."

She shifted from one foot to the other. "Well, I'm pretty sure."

"Not positive?"

Her heart was beating like a drum. She could hardly breathe at all. And while she was trying to find words, he moved forward. He pulled her gently into his arms and bent to kiss her full on the mouth.

She protested once, weakly, but the old, sweet hunger filled her again. His lips probed and teased. Finally, she went on tiptoe to kiss him back, letting her mouth open under his. He trembled wildly, and she felt a burst of warmth at her own power.

He lifted his head and looked down at her like a starving man, oblivious to the amused stares of onlookers. "My God, I've gone out of my mind trying to find you," he murmured huskily. "I never should have let you get away. Well, I've got you now, and I'm not letting go. I don't care about the money, I want you!"

He actually seemed to mean it. Of course, she'd thought Adam meant it, too. She glanced dazedly past him and saw people starting to whisper among themselves.

"Cameron . . ."

"That's how you said my name in bed," he recalled, bending to rest his forehead on hers. "I've relived that night over and over again. Come on, let's go somewhere and talk."

"You don't want to talk," she accused, moving away from contact with his long, hard body.

"Of course I do. Eventually."

"Then you can do it in a crowd," she said in a huff, going to sit on the staircase. "I'm not going to go off and be alone with you."

"I'll let you seduce me again," he coaxed, dropping down beside her.

She flushed and avoided his hot stare. "How are your mother and Amanda?"

"Missing you. Amanda's moped around like an orphan. Mother senses that something happened, but she's been too busy finishing the book to ask. That's why she isn't with me," he added, smiling. "I didn't tell her who the Steeles were."

"Would you have come to find me, if you'd known?" she murmured.

"Yes," he said. He reached out and touched her hair lightly. "I've had little more than memories and dreams to sustain me these past weeks," he said tautly. "The reality of you is shattering. Did you miss me?"

"No," she said curtly, looking away. He was Adam all over again, wanting her for what she had, for what she was. Her eyes closed.

He sighed heavily. "I even know what you're thinking," he said quietly. "I suppose it will take time."

"What will?"

"Convincing you to marry me," he said carelessly. She looked at him, her green eyes wide. "No!"

"Yes." He lifted her slender hand to his mouth and kissed the palm slowly, softly, looking into her eyes.

"You're in love with me, Merlyn. You said so." He sighed roughly. "I'll never get over that as long as I live. I was too shocked to save myself. I let you lead me off like a lamb going to slaughter."

Her face flamed, and she tried to jerk her hand away, but he wouldn't release it. "Some lamb!" she whispered, glancing around to make sure no one was within hearing.

"Merlyn," he said gently, "I've never before let a woman do to me what you did. I suppose it was misplaced pride or masculine arrogance . . . but I always had to be the dominant partner. It was, in a sense, my first time, too."

That pleased her. But the eyes that searched his face were still wary, worried, uncertain.

"I'll woo you, little heiress," he said, "if that's what you want. All of it. Candy, flowers, I'll even serenade you."

"That will be the day," she ground out.

"You don't think I can?" he murmured, smiling slowly. "Ah, but I've changed, Merlyn. I've become uninhibited."

She swallowed hard and tried to avoid his eyes. They were sensual, and the warmth of his big body and its spicy scent were beginning to weaken her.

"I don't want to marry you," she said under her breath.

"We can't let our baby be born illegitimate," he murmured, smiling at her.

"I'm not pregnant!" she burst out.

Beside the staircase, several couples stopped talking and stared at them, aghast.

"Yes, you are!" he said, deliberately raising his

voice. "And it's my baby! Why won't you marry me and give it a name?"

Her face went blood red. "Cameron!"

He stood up slowly, towering over her, his eyes dancing with dark mischief. "Imagine, a well brought up young lady like you refusing to marry the father of her child!"

She got to her feet so quickly she almost fell.

He caught her, holding her gently. "There, now, darling, you have to be careful," he taunted. "We wouldn't want you to hurt the baby."

She tried to speak, but he swung her up into his powerful arms and carried her gently the two steps to the bottom.

"I'd carry you the other way," he murmured wickedly, "but I can't risk dropping you."

"I'll get even with you if . . ." she sputtered.

He smothered the words under his warm, rough mouth, and there were louder murmurs and a few isolated chuckles as he knocked every single protest out of her mind.

"Remember what we did in the closet that night?" he whispered, his mouth poised just above hers. "I'd like to do it with you right now. I'd like to feel your breasts . . ."

"Don't," she moaned, hiding her face in his throat.

He laughed softly. "Marry me, Merlyn."

"No. You only want me for what I have," she said coldly.

"That's a fact," he whispered, brushing his mouth over her eyelids until they closed. "I want you for your mind, and your heart, and for this body that makes me ache every time I touch it."

"That's not what I meant," she groaned.

He met her eyes and looked into them quietly. "I won't take no for an answer. You could be pregnant. We did nothing to prevent it."

Her lips trembled as he slowly put her down on her feet. She looked up at him stubbornly.

"Well, if there is a baby, it's mine," she said.

"Ours," he corrected, with a slow grin.

She stomped her foot. "Cameron!"

He caught her hand and tugged at it. "Come have some punch and calm down. It isn't good for you to get upset, in your condition."

She started to speak and then gave up when she saw the amused glances they were getting. Her jaw clenched. So it was war, was it? Well, he'd better have an arsenal, because he had a fight on his hands. She wasn't going to be his plaything and his purse, all at once. No, sir!

11

How could you do that to me?" she asked her father later, as the party was just beginning to wind down.

He grinned at her, with a wry glance toward Cameron, who'd hardly left her side all evening. "Just playing cupid, darling," he said. "I like him. He'll do me for a son-in-law."

"I thought we'd agreed that you were through playing matchmaker," she said archly.

His eyebrows rose. "I had nothing to do with it," he reminded her.

Her eyes narrowed. "Really? Just how much did you know about Cameron before you helped me find that job with his mother?"

He looked briefly uncomfortable. "Well, actually, I had met him once or twice," he confided. "And I knew he was unmarried. But he was your exact opposite, darling."

"So he was," she agreed, not quite convinced. She sighed angrily. "I'm not going to marry him."

"Oh, of course not," he agreed. He lifted a silvery eyebrow. "Just as a matter of curiosity, how do you plan to stop him?"

"By saying no," she said.

"It won't work."

"And I'm not pregnant!"

Both eyebrows went up. "The certainty of youth," he murmured dryly. "You didn't eat breakfast this morning."

She flushed. "I wasn't hungry!"

"I thought the smell of the bacon put you off?"

"Dad!" she groaned.

"A banker will be a nice addition to my board of directors," he continued, unabashed. "And we can schedule the christening to coincide with the annual report. . . ."

"Will you listen?"

". . . not to mention the wedding." He frowned thoughtfully. "Let's see, it had better be soon. Next week, I think. I'll speak to Cameron."

She stopped in the middle of the floor. "I will not marry him," she said, carefully enunciating every word.

"Don't be silly, of course you will." He smiled at her and beckoned to his future son-in-law.

She hated that smile. She always had. The last time she'd seen it was when she decided to drop out of college.

"She's all yours, son," her father told Cameron, handing her over with a flourish. "There are too many available ladies around tonight for me to spend the entire evening with my own daughter. Lovely though she is," he added with a mocking bow, and strode away.

"A man after my own heart," Cameron murmured with a smile as he led her to the dance floor. "He'll be a good grandfather."

"I am not pregnant. I am not marrying you."

"Come upstairs and let's lie down and discuss it," he said with a twinkle in his dark eyes.

"I was drunk!"

He took her in his arms and moved slowly to the romantic music of a waltz. "No, you were in love. So was I. I tried to do the right thing, but once you pulled off that gown . . ." The smile faded, and his eyes grew dark and fiery. The big arm that was holding her contracted slowly, softly crushing her breasts against his jacket. "Merlyn, without clothes, you are the most beautiful thing I've ever seen."

She flushed and dropped her eyes to his chest. "Stop that."

"Did I please you?" he asked quietly. He tilted her face up. "Did I, darling?"

"You know very well that you did," she groaned, hiding her face against him. "Cam . . ."

His hand slid slowly over the soft skin of her back. "I want you," he whispered softly. "I want to do what we did that night, all over again."

She was trembling. She couldn't help it. The memories were blistering hot. She clenched her fingers on the fabric of his jacket. "I can't."

"Darling, look at me." His soft, dark eyes looked

down at her green ones and smiled into them. "There's no shame in what we did together, Merlyn," he said softly. "As long as we make it right."

"Make it right?"

"Get married," he said. "For the baby's sake."

"Cameron, there isn't a baby!" she burst out.

"I think there is," he returned. His eyes moved down her body and back up again, searching her face. "You're radiant. You glow. As innocent as you were, you couldn't be expected to know—but what happened, what we felt, wasn't quite a common thing." His fingers came up to brush a strand of short hair away from her eye. "Darling, didn't it occur to you that I lost control completely that first time? And didn't you wonder why?"

Her heart was trying to climb out of her throat. He was hypnotizing her all over again, and she couldn't let him!

"You needed a woman," she said bluntly.

He shook his head. "I've needed women before, and that hasn't happened. I wanted you in an uncommon way. And being seduced by virgins isn't an everyday experience for me. The combination blew my mind."

"I don't know what came over me," she whispered.

"I do," he said under his breath. His arm contracted. "I took you, and you took me. And now we've got to do something about it, for the sake of that tiny life we created between us. And don't say you're not pregnant. You are. Merlyn, we loved that night. As intense and beautiful as the experience was," he whispered, "you have to be pregnant."

Her breath caught in her throat, and for an instant she gave in to her longing for him, her aching love for him. "I wanted to be," she whispered huskily.

"I wanted it, too," he whispered. "I wanted it so much that I held nothing back with you."

That was surprising, and her eyes told him so.

"Another shock?" he asked gently. "I could have protected you, Merlyn, if I'd wanted to. I'm not saying it would have been the easiest thing I've ever done, but if I'd been determined to prevent a child, I could have." She stopped dancing, and he touched her lips lightly with his fingertips.

"And you didn't?" she asked.

He held her palm to his lips. "On the contrary," he said in a husky tone. His eyes searched hers. "I tried my damndest to make sure you got pregnant."

"Why?"

"Because I . . ."

Before he could finish the statement, a slightly inebriated Dick brushed against Cameron.

"Sorry, old man—" He grinned, "—but I did have this dance planned. Merlyn, my love?"

He swept her away, oblivious to the killing glare Cameron gave him and the shock on Merlyn's face. People closed in around them just as Cameron started after her; the music got louder; and Merlyn came back to her senses. She had to keep from being alone with Cameron again. If she wanted to salvage any of her pride, she had to! He was only pretending to want her. Probably he'd wanted her to get pregnant for the same reason he wanted to marry her—because he needed money, and she had it. A lot of loose ends didn't fit well into that theory, but she ignored them. She wasn't going to risk her pride again, as she had with Adam.

At the end of the dance she slipped away and hid upstairs until the last guest was leaving. From the deep murmur of his voice, she knew that it was Cameron. The door closed.

"You can come out now," her father called gaily. "He's gone!"

"Can I trust you?" she called after a minute.

"Darling, I'm your doting papa!"

"You're a turncoat," she accused.

"Now, Merlyn."

She came down the stairs, saw no one, and relaxed a little as she moved forward. "Is he gone for good?" she asked.

"Not a chance. He's coming to lunch tomorrow, in fact. We're going to do business."

She glared at him. "Why?"

"Well, seeing he's the father of my grandchild . . ."

"There isn't a grandchild," she moaned. "I'm not pregnant!"

". . . I have to look out for him," he concluded amiably. "Shouldn't you be in bed? Women in your condition need to be careful."

She gave him a killing glare and climbed the stairs again. What was the use of arguing with either one of them? They were cut from the same cloth, and she hated them both!

She dodged Cameron the next day by going shopping, but he was still there when she came home. And so were baskets full of flowers, from one end of the living room to the other.

"The flowers," Cameron offered, grinning at her. He was wearing a white shirt with a yellow sweater and gray slacks, and he looked wickedly handsome.

"What flowers?" she asked nervously.

His eyes were disturbing as they ran down the length of her body. "As in candy, flowers, and serenading."

She cocked her head, determined to sound poised. "What about the candy?"

"It's in your bathtub."

She blinked. "What?"

He turned away and lit a cigarette. "Go look."

With a quick glance at her father, who was trying to stifle a grin, she went cautiously up the staircase and into her bedroom. She opened the bathroom door.

The tub was lined with lace-rimmed red satin and filled to capacity with boxes of chocolates of every kind imaginable. She stood gaping at it for a long minute before she turned and walked back downstairs.

"The best part's still to come," Cameron offered.

"You're going to serenade me?" she asked. Her eyes flashed. "Better have an umbrella handy," she said with a mocking smile.

"Better have a big bucket of water," he returned on a laugh.

She went into the study and locked the door. When she came out, he was gone, but her father had a strange look on his face.

"I'm going to check into a hotel," she announced as she went upstairs to bed. "I am not going to stay here and become a target. Maybe if I leave, he'll go back to Charleston and marry that Delle person!"

"Not a chance," her father replied, laughing.

"Care to bet?" she threw back.

"I'll bet you a Mercedes convertible for a wedding present," he said obligingly.

She turned on her heel and stalked upstairs. This is getting out of hand! she thought. And she felt queasy. The sight of the candy in the tub had unsettled her stomach.

With a sigh, she donned her blue silk nightgown and matching robe and sat down to comb her short hair. That was when she heard the noise. It sounded like an orchestra tuning up.

Frowning, she opened the door to the hall and listened. Yes, there it was again. She smiled. Probably her father was listening to a concert on the educational television channel. She closed the door and went back to the vanity. She'd just lifted the brush again when the opening bars of the *Capriccio espagnol* by Rimsky-Korsakov shattered the night in orchestral splendor.

She cried out. The brush went flying. The orchestra sounded as if it was in the room with her, and she realized suddenly that the music wasn't coming from the hall at all. It was coming from the lawn!

She dashed to the window, opened it, and stepped out onto the balcony. Cameron was standing below, just in front of the conductor, and Merlyn realized with wide-eyed fascination that the entire Atlanta Symphony Orchestra was playing magnificently in her back yard on the neatly clipped lawn!

Cameron bowed, grinned, and blew her a kiss. He was wearing a black tuxedo himself and carrying a violin. As she watched, he raised it to his neck and nodded toward the conductor. As the background music softened, he began to play.

He was terrible. Absolutely terrible. Merlyn gritted her teeth. Several members of the orchestra, especially in the string section, looked as if they were trying to find earplugs.

"Oh, stop!" she wailed.

"Marry me, and I will!" he yelled up.

"Never!"

"It gets worse!" he threatened. "You haven't heard what I can do to a French horn!"

12

⸻⸻⸻⸻

He continued playing. Lights were beginning to go on all around the neighborhood. The people next door poked their heads out of an upstairs window.

"What's that horrible noise?" somebody yelled.

Cameron paused, violin and bow in hand, and glared in the direction of the voice. "I'll have you know I studied violin for two years!" he yelled back.

"Yes," the voice answered, "right up until your teacher committed suicide!"

Cameron drew the bow across the helpless violin strings with a vengeance.

"Please stop!" the voice yelled. "If you're the enemy, I surrender!"

"I don't take prisoners!" Cameron shouted.

"In that case, buy some armor!" the voice threatened.

Merlyn was laughing almost hysterically at the exchange. She could hardly believe the evidence of her own eyes and ears. If only Delle could see him now, she thought wickedly. Cameron Thorpe, staid bank executive. She giggled even more.

"Well, are you going to marry me or not?" he yelled up at her.

"I'll keep an open mind!" she called down, clutching the thin robe around her. "Cameron, I have to go in. I'm cold!"

"Go ahead!" he called up. "We wouldn't want the baby to get sick!"

She glared at him, then went in and closed the balcony doors. Minutes later, when she was tucked in bed, the exquisite strains of the famous Brahms lullaby filled the house. And the yard. And the neighborhood. And then there was the ominous sound of a police siren. . . .

Sunlight streamed in the window and awakened Merlyn. She stretched and sat up with a sigh. With the end of sleep came memory, and she laughed. Only a madman would hire an entire symphony orchestra to accompany his pathetic serenade, she decided. But a lovely madman.

She got out of bed, feeling faintly queasy, and went to get a drink of water. Then she dressed in jeans and a blouse and went downstairs.

Cameron was sitting at the breakfast table with her father, looking half-asleep. He was wearing tan slacks and a striped, open-throated shirt, and he looked as rakish as a particularly sexy pirate. The open neck of the shirt displayed tanned skin and the beginnings of a thick pelt of hair. She remembered the feel of that hair against her bare skin and went weak-kneed with memory. Her eyes met his dark ones, and he lifted an eyebrow at her smile.

"Feeling good, are we?" he taunted.

"My, someone's sour this morning," she returned, bending to kiss her father's forehead as she passed him.

"You'd be sour, too, if you'd spent the night in a police station," Cameron sighed, sipping his coffee. "Don't I get a kiss, too? After all, I'm the father of your child."

"I am not pregnant!" she ground out.

"Have some bacon," her father interrupted with a wicked grin, and offered her the platter.

She swallowed and averted her eyes.

"As I was saying," Cameron continued, chuckling, "how about my kiss?"

"You can't refuse him," her father observed. "After all, he was arrested on your behalf."

She stared at her father, aghast. "I didn't ask him to stand outside my window and make those horrible noises!"

"They were not horrible," Cameron defended himself.

"Of course not, to the tone-deaf," she agreed. She smiled impishly. "It was kind of sweet, though."

He cocked a heavy eyebrow. "Does that mean you're going to marry me?"

Her father cleared his throat, stood, and put down his napkin. "I have just remembered a pressing appointment somewhere," he announced. "I should be back around dark, if anyone calls."

"You're going to be a super father-in-law," Cameron observed.

"You bet I am." Her father grinned and winked at them. "By the way, just in case there's anything to celebrate, I've made a reservation at Chez Moi for tonight. See you!"

Chez Moi was a very elegant, wildly expensive French restaurant on Peachtree Street. Merlyn stared at Cameron with narrowed eyes.

"Confident, isn't he?" she asked deliberately.

"Yes, he is," he agreed. He searched her eyes. "Sadly, a hell of a lot more confident than I am." He sipped his black coffee and put the dainty china cup back in its saucer. "Don't you think it's time we sat down together to discuss things?"

She started to make light of it, but his eyes were dark and quiet, and she thought better of it. The way she was beginning to feel was no joke.

"All right," she said after a minute.

He took her hand and led her out through the patio door, into the morning sun. It was warm outside, and the tall oak trees provided abundant shade. Interspersed around the yard were beautiful pink and white dogwood trees, in full bloom. A birdbath with three tiers and a fountain splashed noisily in the midst of blooming shrubs.

Cameron's fingers fit themselves between hers in an intimate, possessive gesture. His hand was big, a little callused, and very strong. She liked its strength.

Her eyes darted up to his broad, hard face and searched it quietly.

"Are you going to marry me?" he asked.

"Because I might be pregnant?"

His fingers contracted and he smiled ruefully. "That," he said, "is probably a pipe dream. I was grasping at straws. But we could make it real, Merlyn. We could get married and build a life together."

He drew her closer and pressed her open palms to his chest. "I know you think it's only because of your money," he said. "But if you'll ask your father about our business deal, you might discover that I'm slowly and surely erasing my father's debt. I won't lie to you, I'm not a wealthy man. I'm well-to-do and not much more. But," he added with a grin, "I'm ambitious and stubborn and I've got prospects. I'll make it. We'll make it."

She stared up at him, hesitant.

He sighed and framed her face with his hands. "Merlyn, if I were poor, with no money and no prospect of having any, would you love me less?" he asked pointedly.

That shocked her. Her eyes scanned his face—his black eyes, his jutting brow. "Oh, no," she confessed softly. She reached up a hand to trace the line of his lips. "No, I wouldn't care what you had. I never have."

"Then why can't you believe that I want you for yourself?" he asked. "I wouldn't care if you were poor, either. It wouldn't matter. If it will convince you," he added, "have your father disinherit you. Then we'll get married and raise children and see if we can build our bank into the biggest in the state."

"You're serious!" she burst out.

"Of course I'm serious," he said with failing patience. His eyes grew, if possible, even blacker and his arms went around her suddenly, crushing her body into his. "My God, can't you see it? For an intelligent woman . . . Merlyn, for God's sake, I love you!"

Her eyes dilated until they looked like saucers. "Me?"

"You, you crazy, outlandish, flamboyant little seductress," he growled. "You teased me and tempted me until I couldn't even add a column of figures without seeing you, and I've chased you and done everything but beg, and I still can't make you see!" His eyes closed. "Merlyn, I'll do anything short of murder to get you. Didn't the orchestra recital tell you anything? Damn it, I've stopped wearing musk cologne— haven't you had a sniff of me yet? I doused myself with British Sterling before I came over here. I've traded in my black car for a red one. I've got new shirts—stripes and colors, and new ties . . . !"

Her fingers against his mouth stopped the passionate tirade. She smiled slowly, lovingly, as it all began to make sense. "If I agree to marry you," she said, "will you let me seduce you once in a while?"

His chest rose and fell heavily. "Any time you like," he agreed.

"And you won't make fun of me if I wear outlandish clothes once in a while?"

He shook his head.

Her hands spread out over his chest in a lazy, caressing motion. "And is Delle out of the picture forever?"

"Delle was out of the picture the night I met you," he breathed. He bent and passed his lips lazily over her closed eyelids. "I wanted you on sight. And it got steadily worse. At that party, when we were dancing, I thought I'd go mad if I couldn't kiss you. Did you think I made a habit of dragging women into closets?"

"No," she admitted. She looked up at him. "Cam, you don't have to go overboard with it. I don't want to change you. I just want you to let me be myself. If you love me, that's all that matters. That's everything."

"I love you, all right," he murmured huskily. His arms tightened. "Oh, God, I do love you so! And that night after you'd been so wild in my arms, you walked out the door with that damned drummer and wouldn't even look at me!"

"And there you were, kissing Delle!" she grumbled.

"Trying to forget you," he admitted, watching her. "And it didn't work. She was afraid I'd muss her hair or smudge her lipstick. It was your mouth I was kissing, anyway. Delle hasn't half the passion you have, my darling."

"I was so afraid that night," she whispered fervently, meeting his gaze. "I wanted you, you see. I ran out with Dick because I was so vulnerable, and I was sure I couldn't say no to you. He's just a friend; that's all there's ever been between us."

He smiled slowly. "I'm glad to know that." He traced her nose with his finger. "That night . . . were you trying to compete with Delle, when you led me into the bedroom and had your way with me?"

She nodded. "Yes, I think I was," she murmured. She laughed shyly. "I never believed I could do that with a man." Her eyes lowered to his chest. "But I thought you were going to marry Delle, as you'd said you were, and that one night with you was all I could ever expect. I wanted it to be a night to remember."

"Which it damned well was. I've been living on it for

the past few weeks. If you knew," he murmured huskily, "how I felt when I called home the next day to apologize, to see if I could make you understand what I felt, and Mother said you were gone . . . God! And then I couldn't find you. No one seemed to know where Miss Forrest had gone." His hands caught her and crushed her into the hard lines of his body. "I was out of my mind by the time your father called and told me the truth. I could have gone on my knees."

"I felt like that when you walked through my front door," she confessed. Her arms slid around him, and she savored the hard muscles of his back. "You really changed your mind about marrying Delle after the first night I spent at the lake?"

"Yes," he replied. He chuckled. "And especially after I kissed you in the closet," he said. "After that, I couldn't work up the least bit of enthusiasm for her. I realized I couldn't really marry for money. It didn't help that both my mother and my daughter kept harping on your assets all the time. They're still at it, by the way," he added with a laugh. "They're wild to come and see you."

She nuzzled her face against his chest. "You could have brought them with you."

"Yes, I could have. But I thought we needed time to ourselves to get this settled."

She nipped at his chest with her teeth.

He caught his breath sharply. "Merlyn!"

She undid the buttons on his shirt easily. She kissed him there, loving the scent of his big body. "You've had a bath," she whispered. "You smell of soap as well as British Sterling."

His hands were clenched at her back. "Yes," he said

in a husky undertone. "Darling, that . . . disturbs me."

"Yes, I know it does," she agreed. She drew back with sultry eyes and led him toward the pool off the patio, which was enclosed by a privacy fence all around and shielded from the house.

He went with her without a protest, and she laughed softly, delightedly, locking the gate before she shoved him down onto the lounger.

"Now, I've got you," she murmured, joining him.

He reached up and tangled his fingers in her hair. His face was soft with love, and his eyes were blazing with new passion. "Have you?"

He moved sharply, turning so that she was under him, and his mouth found hers in one smooth, hungry motion.

She gasped at the unleashed ferocity, at the sudden, swift intrusion of his hands under her blouse.

"Yes," he whispered ardently, lifting his head to watch with glittering eyes as he discovered the lack of undergarments under the soft blouse. His hands stroked her taut breasts, his thumbs nudging the hardened nubs insistently, his chest rising and falling with shuddering breaths. "Yes, you want me, don't you?"

"Want you?" she breathed raggedly. "I'd die for you!"

His hands moved again, and one of them lifted to rip open the buttons, baring her swollen breasts to his eyes. He bent and put his open mouth against the very tip of one, slowly taking it until he all but enveloped her in the moist, warm caress. She arched gracefully, and caught his head in her hands, to urge it closer.

"It was like this," she whispered softly, "that night was like this. I wanted you so much, and I was afraid you'd push me away."

"I couldn't have lived if I'd done that," he confessed. "I wanted you too much. But I felt so bad afterwards. You were a virgin, and I'd let my heart rule my head. I was sure you'd hate me for it."

She held his face in her hands and stared at him incredulously. "So that's why you were acting so strange!"

He smiled ruefully. "I thought it was the wine," he said. "That you'd overindulged and given in to lust. I didn't really believe you loved me. Not until I had time to think about it, that is. Then I remembered what you'd said before, and what you'd told me the day we walked in the woods, about only being able to give yourself in love, and forever." He bent and brushed his mouth over hers lovingly. "But by the time I remembered, you were gone. Oh, God, I thought I'd lost you," he whispered as he took her mouth. He crushed it under his, and the whole weight of his body came down on her, his hair-matted chest crushing her soft, bare breasts, his hips insistent and disturbing over her own, his thighs parting hers with sheer weight.

Her fingers clung to him, loving the heaviness of his body, the intimacy of the embrace. She returned the kiss as wildly as he gave it, her mouth open and inviting, her tongue eager and ardent.

He lifted his head eventually, and he was as flushed and wild-eyed as she was.

"I love you," he ground out harshly. "Now do you marry me, or . . . ?"

"Yes, I'll marry you," she whispered. She reached up with a long sigh, and touched his hard mouth. "Today, tomorrow, any time you say. On one condition," she added with mock solemnity.

He lifted an eyebrow. "What?"

"That you stop playing the violin forever!"

He chuckled. "Well, I suppose we can let one of the kids take lessons, later."

She smiled secretly and drew him slowly down to her. "Yes, darling," she whispered. "One of the kids. Cam, I love you," she breathed into his mouth.

He smiled back and kissed her thoroughly. His head lifted slowly, and he looked down at her with possessive eyes. "Merlyn, all kidding aside, is there going to be a baby?" he asked.

She stretched lazily and looped her arms around his neck. "I truly don't know. But it's very possible."

He nuzzled her nose with his. "If you aren't pregnant yet, we can always try again," he whispered. His hips moved slowly over hers, and his eyes burned down into her wide, loving ones. "How do you feel about making love under the sun?"

Her lips parted. "Here?" she whispered, glancing around.

The hands against her bare skin were becoming urgent. "Right here," he whispered.

Her fingers smoothed over his broad chest, and she savored the feel of his muscles, his immediate reaction to her. He wanted her desperately, she could feel it. And she wanted him. His body was like a narcotic: it made her dizzy with longing; it made her ache in the oddest places.

He lifted himself just a little so that he could look down on her uncovered breasts, and he stared at them hungrily. "Shy?" he murmured wickedly.

"Someone might come by," she faltered. "The maid, or the gardener . . . or Dad . . ."

"And you say I'm conservative," he chided. He chuckled softly as his hand went to the top of her jeans and slowly moved the zipper down. "You just locked the gate," he whispered.

"Cam!"

But his mouth had already taken possession of hers, and his hands were skillfully easing her out of her clothing. She felt the warmth of the sun like a kiss on her smooth, bare skin. "Your father gave the hired help the day off," he whispered into her open mouth. "Didn't you know? And he told me he was locking the main gate on the way out." He lifted his head. "Look around. Only the birds could see us here."

That was probably true, but while she was looking around, he was getting the rest of the fabric out of the way, and when she started to frame another question, it was far too late.

Her voice splintered as he parted her lips with the urgent pressure of his. His hands were touching, guiding, his body moving warmly, hungrily against hers in an arousing rhythm. His chest brushed against her breasts with an abrasiveness that was wildly ardent.

"That's it," he whispered as she began to move under his weight. "Yes, darling, yes, yes!"

She moaned as the pleasure began to build, and her fingers moved all over him, soothing, caressing, inciting, until they found his hips and urged him closer. Her eyes opened and she looked up through a mist of desire, seeing the hard intensity of passion on his face.

"Cameron," she whispered shakily.

His nostrils flared, his eyes flickered. He lifted his torso and moved his hips slowly against her. As he did, his eyes wandered possessively over every slender inch of her. "I've been too long without you," he breathed roughly.

"Oh, I've missed you so," she whispered. She arched her body toward his, her eyes burning, her face taut with passion, with the knowledge that this was truly love, not just a physical release.

His eyes went back to hers and he eased himself down again, his movements urgent now, hard, rough.

"Yes," she whispered, matching her own passion to his. "Yes!"

"We're loving, this time," he ground out as his hands clutched her hips. He held her eyes hungrily. "Loving, Merlyn!"

"Loving!" she whispered back, her voice shaking. Her body seemed to have a will of its own, matching the reckless passion of his, and she closed her eyes as new sensations drove reality out of her mind. She shifted and suddenly cried out as wave after wave of pleasure buffeted her. She clung to him, wrapped herself around him, possessing him as his body completed its hungry invasion. She wanted to please him in every way he'd pleased her, with her hands, her mouth. . . . Her efforts were rewarded with the hoarse, harsh cry that came from his throat and mingled softly with the musical whistling of songbirds and the distant sound of traffic.

Trembling, he lifted his head and looked down at her with passionate black eyes. After a minute, he began to kiss her, his mouth tender now, deliciously tender and loving.

She clung, indulging him, brushing her trembling mouth over his closed eyelids. "Oh, my," she whispered unsteadily.

"Yes," he murmured. "Oh, my. So good, so gloriously sweet . . . loving. This is what it should be."

"Wild honey," she whispered, laughing a little.

"It was wild, all right." He lifted his head to look at her, smiling softly. "Thank you. Did I ever say thank you?"

"For what?" she asked gently.

"For saving all this for me. For not giving in to anyone who asked, for not belonging to the sexually permissive world out there. For coming to me a virgin."

She caught her breath. "I'm glad I waited, Cam," she said quietly. "You know, honestly, if I had it all to do over again, I think I wouldn't have drunk so much wine and seduced you." She smiled ruefully. "It still feels uncomfortable, without marriage."

"Yes, I know," he said quietly, watching her. "Tomorrow we'll put it right; we'll be married as soon as possible and ease your guilty conscience. I suppose it's different for a woman. But I do love you, Merlyn. With all my heart."

She brushed her lips against his. "I love you, too."

He sat up slowly, stretching, and she stared at him wonderingly. His body was as muscular and perfect as a Greek statue, rippling and shadowed with dark hair. "You're beautiful, Cam," she whispered shakily.

"I'm glad you think so," he replied, his eyes warm and soft with love and fulfillment. They ran up and down her slender body, lingering on the slight swell of her stomach, the high perfection of her breasts. "I'll have to find another word for you. Beautiful doesn't come close."

She got to her feet, still trembling a little, and let him draw her into a warm, close embrace. She nuzzled her face against his damp, hairy chest. "By the swimming pool!" She laughed softly. "And I used to think you were so conventional."

He nibbled at her ear. "I was. Until you came along and shook my world to its foundations with your wild clothes and wilder mouth. I think we may die someday trying to satisfy each other in bed."

She sighed and closed her eyes. "Oh, darling, but what a way to go."

And he didn't argue with that.

By the time Jared Steele came back home late that afternoon, they were sitting on the front porch dressed to the hilt, waiting for him so that they could have supper at Chez Moi.

He came dancing up the steps and grinned at Merlyn's soft white chiffon dress and Cameron's tuxedo. "Give me two shakes and I'll have my tux on. By the way, are we celebrating?"

Cameron grinned, holding Merlyn's hand warmly in his. "We certainly are."

"Go ahead, gloat," Merlyn muttered, glaring up at her parent. "Say 'I told you so.'"

His silvery eyebrows arched. "Who, me? But I had nothing to do with it."

"Oh yes you did," she returned. "You talked me into playing the part of an ordinary working girl, and you knew Cameron didn't have a wife. You sneaky old devil."

Her father put his hand to his heart. "I am not sneaky. Cameron, did I know you before this all came up?"

Cameron pursed his firm lips. "Well, we did have lunch together at that last business conference, and you did pump me for the story of my life."

"When?" Merlyn asked.

"About a week before you went to work for Mother." Cameron grinned. "Of course, I had no idea whose father he was at the time."

"Dad!" she burst out.

"How was I to know the two of you would hit it off?" Jared asked innocently.

She sighed angrily. "Well, at least you won't be doing any more matchmaking now," she said smugly.

"Think not?" The older man grinned and started into the house. "Wait until your children come along."

"Dad!" she cried after him.

Wicked, soft laughter floated out to the porch as she met Cameron's dancing eyes.

"What are we going to do about him?" she asked with a resigned sigh.

He grinned as he caught her fingers and locked them in his. He leaned back against the glider and stretched. "No problem, darling," he said lazily. "I know this lovely middle-aged widow in Jonesboro who has four unmarried sisters. . . ."

She burst out laughing. As the sun melted down behind the sheltering oak trees, she looked up into Cameron's eyes and saw everything she would ever want or need in their dark, loving depths.

Silhouette Desire

A new romance series
that explores
contemporary relationships
in exciting detail

*And now, you can order the books
written by your favorite authors!*

Nora Powers
_____ PROMISE ME TOMORROW   No. 33/$1.95
_____ DREAM OF THE WEST   No. 48/$1.95
_____ TIME STANDS STILL   No. 59/$2.25

Kathryn Mallory
_____ A FRENCHMAN'S KISS   No. 6/$1.95
_____ GENTLE CONQUEST   No. 40/$1.95
_____ ONE NIGHT'S DECEPTION   No. 58/$2.25

Suzanne Michelle
_____ ENCHANTED DESERT   No. 29/$1.95
_____ SILVER PROMISES   No. 47/$1.95
_____ NO PLACE FOR A WOMAN   No. 57/$2.25

Rita Clay
_____ WISE FOLLY   No. 3/$1.95
_____ YESTERDAY'S DREAMS   No. 32/$1.95
_____ EXPERIMENT IN LOVE   No. 45/$1.95

Silhouette Desire
**320 Steelcase Rd. E., Markham,
Ontario L3R 2M1**

Please send me the books I have checked above. I am enclosing a total of $_____ (Please add 75 cents for postage & handling.) My cheque or money order is enclosed. (No cash or C.O.D.'s please.)

Name_____

Address_____ Apt._____

City_____

Prov. _____ Postal Code_____

Prices subject to change without notice.   (DBD1)

Silhouette Intimate Moments
Receive 2 Books Free!

Free-Books Certificate
MAIL TODAY To Reserve Your Home Subscription

Silhouette BOOK CLUB OF CANADA
320 Steelcase Rd. E., Markham, Ont. L3R 2M1

YES, please send me FREE, and without obligation, 2 exciting Silhouette paperback originals. Unless you hear from me after I receive my 2 FREE BOOKS, please send me 4 full-length, Silhouette Intimate Moments novels to preview each month, as soon as they are published. I understand that you will bill me just $2.50 each (a total of $10.00) with *no additional shipping, handling or other hidden charges.* There is no minimum number of books that I must buy, and I can cancel this arrangement anytime I wish. The first 2 books are mine to keep, even if I never take a single additional book.

Signature_____
(If under 18, parent or guardian must sign)

Name_____

Address_____

City_____

Prov. _____ Postal Code_____

2 FREE BOOKS NOW...
4 BOOKS DELIVERED RIGHT
TO YOUR HOME!

*This offer limited to one per household, expires March 31, 1985. If price changes
are necessary, you will be notified.*

IM2FD